PROTECT YOUR QUEEN

QUEEN #1

PENELOPE SKY

HARTWICK PUBLISHING

Hartwick Publishing
Protect Your Queen
Copyright © 2017 by Penelope Sky
All Rights Reserved

CONTENTS

CREWE

Handcuffed and sporting a black eye, Joseph Ingram sat in the black chair with his hands bound behind his back. The left side of his lip was swollen from a powerful fist, and his tailored suit possessed holes from the burning end of a cigarette. Two of his men flanked him on either side, just as bloodied as he was.

Stirling Castle was so ancient my mind couldn't comprehend it. Built in the 12th century, my Scottish ancestors lived in luxury. Times had changed, but the family line had remained intact. I was the owner of this fine landmark, but its sole purpose was for business endeavors.

Like this one.

I entered the room in my black suit with matching black tie. My silver cufflinks caught the dim light as I took my seat across the table from Joseph, a man I despised immensely. When it came to business, personal opinion was irrelevant. Whoever paid the right price was entitled to whatever I had to offer.

But this man made the mistake of betraying me.

He couldn't meet my gaze, afraid of my wrath. Foolish for thinking he would get away with it, he was now at my mercy. I could do anything I wanted, and he knew it. I could kill him and bury him in the graveyard where my ancient ancestors rotted. I could cut up his body and drop the pieces off the coast.

Joseph bowed his head slightly, as if the muscles of his neck couldn't keep his head upright. He reminded me of a baby, too weak to carry his own weight.

I crossed my legs under the table and unbuttoned the front of my suit. One hand rested on my propped-up knee as I examined my foe, this idiot with an ego too big to handle. I traded him some valuable intelligence for a premium price—four million dollars.

But he didn't pay up.

Instead, he gave me counterfeit bills.

Like I wouldn't have figured it out. "You insulted me, Joseph."

The second I spoke, he flinched slightly. He adjusted his body in the chair, and no matter how much he tried to hide it, he shook. I spotted the tremble in his arms, the shake of his extremities.

"And you know what I do to people who insult me."

He cleared his throat, his Adam's apple moving as he swallowed. "Crewe—"

"Mr. Donoghue." Dunbar was my right-hand man, serving out his life in voluntary servitude. I saved his life and gave him the vengeance he deserved. As a result, he devoted his life to serving me—loyally.

Joseph cringed at the false move. "Mr. Donoghue, I'm sorry."

I chuckled because he was making it worse. "Don't apologize. Men like us don't apologize for our wrongdoings. We have every intent of lying, stealing, and misleading our victims. Own up to it—like man."

Joseph fell quiet, knowing he was out of excuses.

"I'll respect you more for it."

Joseph finally looked at me, his brown eyes showing his weakness. "I'll double the amount I owe you. Eight million. Just let me go."

"Now we're talking." I adjusted the sleeve of my suit, meticulous about my appearance, like always. I wore power like a fresh suit, filling out the clothing as if it were made for me. An invisible crown sat upon my head, something I balanced at all times.

"I can get it to you in twenty-four hours," he said. "All in cash. Just let us go."

"A tempting offer." Now that we'd cut to the chase, things were a lot more interesting.

"Do we have a deal?" He adjusted his arms to get comfortable. The bite of the metal around his wrists must have been painful.

I gazed at his two cronies, both equally unimpressive. While they were burly with muscle, they didn't have true strength and agility. Their eyes hinted at stupidity, following orders without understanding what they were doing. That's how they got into this mess in the first place —because their boss was even dumber. "Money doesn't mean anything to me, Joseph. Reputation is everything."

His eyes fell with devastation. "I'll make it twelve million."

The corner of my mouth rose in a smile. "You need to learn how to listen."

His rate of breathing increased, his chest rising and falling with his impending doom.

"I have an image to maintain. If I let you off the hook that easily, my other business partners won't hesitate to cross me. Obviously, I can't allow this."

"Don't kill me…" His voice shook in desperation. "I made a mistake. You've made mistakes too."

"But it wasn't a mistake." Now my voice deepened, my anger slowly growing to enormous proportions. "You aren't a child, Joseph. You understood what you were doing when you did it. Your only mistake was the idiotic belief that you could get away with it."

He bowed his head, his chest moving at a quicker pace.

"I don't accept your money. However, I'm going to let you go."

Joseph raised his head slowly, his eyes meeting mine with incredulity.

I had the perfect compensation for what he had done, something you couldn't put a price on. I had no remorse for what I had done. It was my responsibility to make an example of my enemies—and I did it well. "I've stolen something from you worth more than money. I've taken something innocent—something pure. And you'll never get it back."

Now Joseph began to shake for entirely different reasons.

"I've taken your lovely sister, London. Now she's mine." I tilted my head and watched his expression, knowing his reaction would be utterly priceless. "She's on her way here now—to become my prisoner."

Joseph's jaw clenched before his eyes widened to the size of baseballs. He burst out of his seat like an angry bronco coming out of the chute. His forehead bulged with a thick vein and his face reddened to the color of a beet. "You motherfucker—"

PROTECT YOUR QUEEN | 7

Dunbar slugged him in the gut and slammed him back down into the chair. He punched him in the mouth for the insult he'd just unleashed my way. "Watch what you say to Mr. Donoghue. Might be your last words." He stood behind Joseph ominously, his arms crossed over his chest.

Joseph clenched his jaw again, frustrated. He was completely helpless to do anything, and that made his rage burn more brightly. His only family member in the world had been taken from him, and he had to sit there and play nice.

I almost felt bad for him—almost. "Would you rather me kill you?"

For an instant, his anger vanished as he considered the question. "Absolutely."

I cocked my head to the side, intrigued by the selfless response. Men like us used others as bulletproof vests, allowing a pile of victims to form around us so we remained untouched. But Joseph didn't hesitate before he gave me his answer. "Then I made the right decision."

The vein in his forehead bulged once more. His arms shook as he tried to break the chain of his handcuffs with only his strength. "She has nothing to do with this. Please, leave her alone."

Joseph finally stood up, his cronies following suit. Dunbar and the rest of my men escorted them outside while I remained in my chair. I didn't see him off, and once he was behind me, I didn't look back. My back was vulnerable and completely exposed, yet I didn't have a single care in the world.

Because whatever attack he made would miss the mark.

Module _____8_____   **Topic** _____(iii)_____

Lies die Wörter und male die Bilder:

der Zahn	der Arm	das Knie
das Auge	der Fuß	das Ohr
der Bauch	der Hals	die Nase

Module_____ **Topic**_____

<u>Hör zu und kreuz das richtige Bild an:_____</u>

Module _____ 8 _____ **Topic** _____ (ii) _____

Hör zu und kreuz das richtige Bild an:

Blank activity and game templates

Game templates

Template   1   Pelmanism/Snap/Beetle
             2   Dominoes
             3a   Noughts and crosses (grid)
             3b   Noughts and crosses
             4a   Wordsearch (10 x 10)
             4b   Wordsearch (14 x 14)
             5a   Battleships (A–E, 1–5)
             5b   Battleships (blank for pictures)
Example   1   Pelmanism/Snap
             2   Beetle
             3   Dominoes
             4   Wordsearch
             5   Battleships

Additional activity/resource templates

Template   6   ID cards
             7   Speech bubbles
             8   Clock
             9   Likes/dislikes
             10   Survey sheet
                     Example survey sheet
             11   Going to Germany, Austria or
                     Switzerland
             12a–c Shop names
             13a,b Days of the week
             14   Girls' names and boys' names
             15a,b Numbers
             16   Alphabet
             17   Family tree
             18   Listening and sorting

Bingo templates

Template B1   School bag (for classroom objects)
             B2   Garden (for animals)
             B3–5 Timetables (for school subjects)
             B6   House (for furniture)
             B7   Basket (for food)
             B8   Snack menu (for food and drinks)
             B9   Town plan (for places in the town)
             B10 Tablecloth (for laying the table)
             B11 Case (for clothes)
             B12 Body (for parts of the body)
            B13 Palette (for colours)

Pelmanism/Snap/Beetle

Dominoes

Noughts and crosses

1	2	3
4	5	6
7	8	9

                                    DEUTSCH? KEIN PROBLEM!

Noughts and crosses

O X

O X

O X X

O O X

Wordsearch 10 X 10

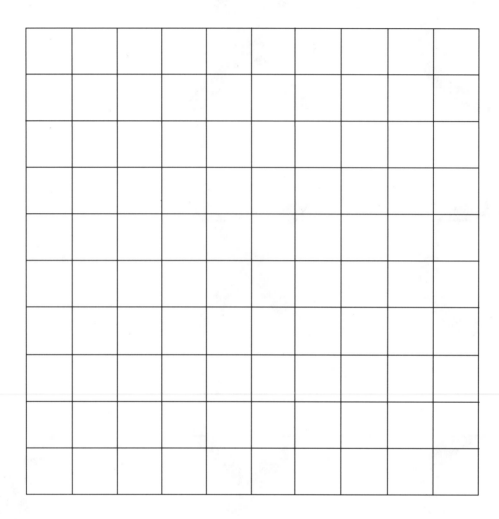

   DEUTSCH? KEIN PROBLEM!

Wordsearch 14 X 14

49

Battleships

	1	2	3	4	5
E					
D					
C					
B					
A					

Battleships

Example 1

Pelmanism/Snap
These need sets of picture and corresponding word cards, preferably on different coloured card.

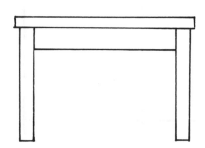

der Tisch

das Sofa

der kleiderschrank

die Gardinen

    DEUTSCH? KEIN PROBLEM!

Example 2

Beetle

This needs sets of six pictures, numbered on the reverse, and a die. A 'banker's card', showing the six items and their die value, will help pupils ask for what they need.

1 = die Shorts
2 = der Pullover
3 = die Jeans
4 = die Socken
5 = die Schuhe
6 = der Rock

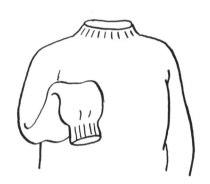

2	1
4	3
6	5

Example 3

Dominoes

das Café	das Museum	die Schule	der Supermarkt	das Haus
der Hafen	das Stadion	der Park	das Schwimmbad	die Disko
das Kino	das Theater	die Altstadt	der Markt	das Eisstadion

Example 4

Wordsearch 10 X 10

B	o	n	t	i	n	K	l	e	i
s	m	B	o	n	b	o	n	s	a
K	M	a	o	T	f	s	b	f	u
l	o	k	C	p	n	m	e	g	a
e	n	i	D	h	H	e	a	u	s
i	K	a	s	s	e	t	t	e	n
d	P	s	m	o	t	i	V	e	k
e	S	b	s	v	s	k	t	d	l
r	e	l	t	e	r	a	ä	n	i
G	e	s	c	h	e	n	k	e	c

Bonbons

Kleider

Kassetten

Geschenke

CDs

Kosmetika

Example 5

Battleships

	Katrin	Wolfgang	Elmar	Heike	Birgit
Pferd					
Maus					
Katze					
Goldfisch					
Hund					

ID cards

Name........................ Vorname.................

Alter................

Adresse...

....

Name........................ Vorname.................

Alter................

Adresse...

....

Speech bubbles

         59

Clock

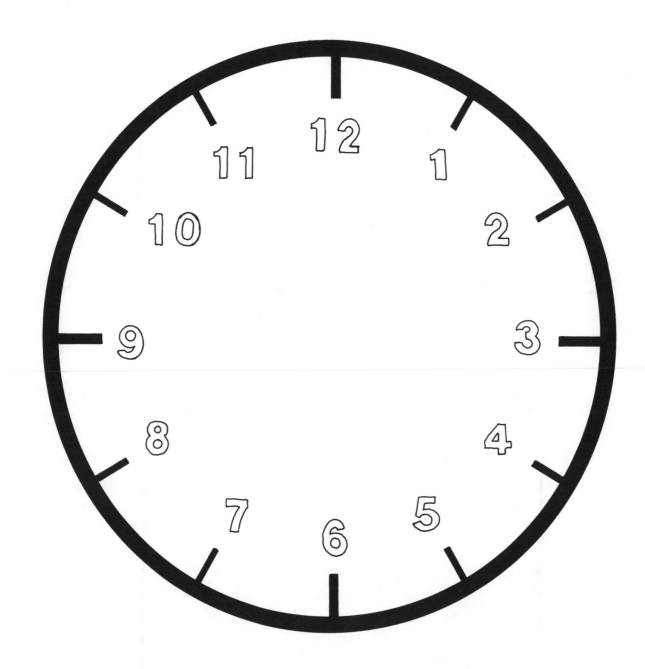

Likes/dislikes

Ich mag

Ich ...... gern

Ich mag nicht

Ich ...... nicht gern

Survey sheet

                              DEUTSCH? KEIN PROBLEM!

Example 10

Survey sheet

Donna						
Kerry						
Alan						
Shane						

Going to Germany, Austria or Switzerland

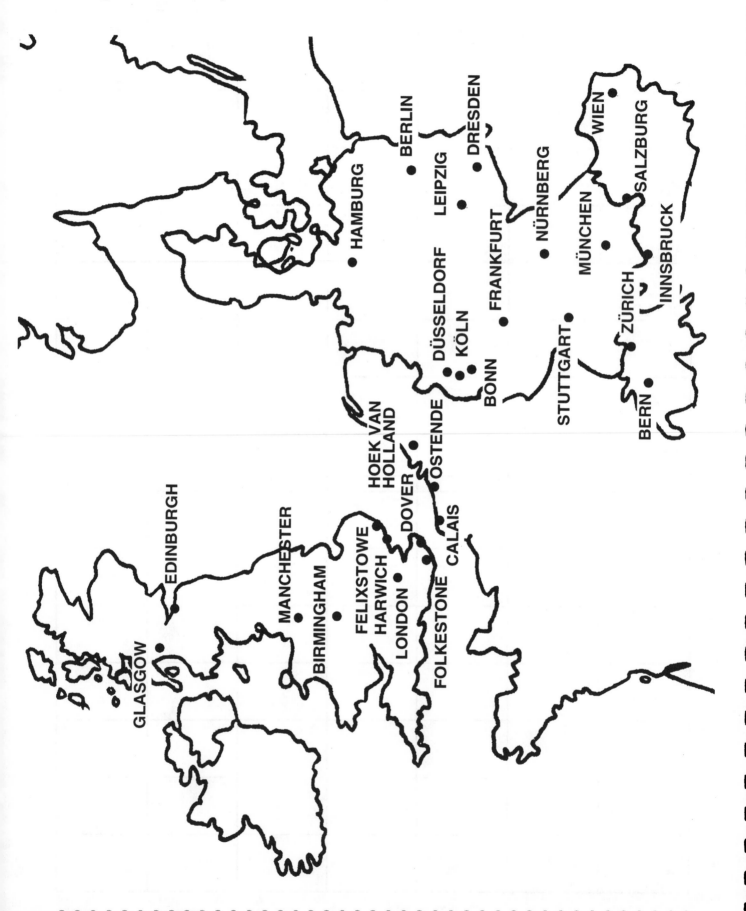

Shop names

die Metzgerei

die Bäckerei

die Apotheke

die Konditorei

Shop names

das Geschäft

das Einkaufszentrum

der Laden

Shop names

der Markt

der Supermarkt

der Zeitungsladen

Days of the week

Montag

Dienstag

Mittwoch

Donnerstag

Days of the week

Freitag

Samstag

Sonntag

Some German girls' names	Some German boys' names
Anna	Andreas
Birgit	Arno
Carola	Bernd
Claudia	Carsten
Hanna	Christian
Heike	Dirk
Jutta	Elmar
Karin	Gerd
Katrin	Jan
Kerstin	Jürgen
Manuela	Markus
Marion	Matthias
Monika	Peter
Petra	Ralf
Sabine	Thomas
Sandra	Wolfgang
Silke	
Tanja	
Ulla	

Numbers 1–31

0	null	16	sechzehn
1	eins	17	siebzehn
2	zwei	18	achtzehn
3	drei	19	neunzehn
4	vier	20	zwanzig
5	fünf	21	einundzwanzig
6	sechs	22	zweiundzwanzig
7	sieben	23	dreiundzwanzig
8	acht	24	vierundzwanzig
9	neun	25	fünfundzwanzig
10	zehn	26	sechsundzwanzig
11	elf	27	siebenundzwanzig
12	zwölf	28	achtundzwanzig
13	dreizehn	29	neunundzwanzig
14	vierzehn	30	dreißig
15	fünfzehn	31	einunddreißig

Numbers 32–100

32 zweiunddreißig	55 fünfundfünfzig	78 achtundsiebzig
33 dreiunddreißig	56 sechsundfünfzig	79 neunundsiebzig
34 vierunddreißig	57 siebenundfünfzig	80 achtzig
35 fünfunddreißig	58 achtundfünfzig	81 einundachtzig
36 sechsunddreißig	59 neunundfünfzig	82 zweiundachtzig
37 siebenunddreißig	60 sechzig	83 dreiundachtzig
38 achtunddreißig	61 einundsechzig	84 vierundachtzig
39 neununddreißig	62 zweiundsechzig	85 fünfundachtzig
40 vierzig	63 dreiundsechzig	86 sechsundachtzig
41 einundvierzig	64 vierundsechzig	87 siebenundachtzig
42 zweiundvierzig	65 fünfundsechzig	88 achtundachtzig
43 dreiundvierzig	66 sechsundsechzig	89 neunundachtzig
44 vierundvierzig	67 siebenundsechzig	90 neunzig
45 fünfundvierzig	68 achtundsechzig	91 einundneunzig
46 sechsundvierzig	69 neunundsechzig	92 zweiundneunzig
47 siebenundvierzig	70 siebzig	93 dreiundneunzig
48 achtundvierzig	71 einundsiebzig	94 vierundneunzig
49 neunundvierzig	72 zweiundsiebzig	95 fünfundneunzig
50 fünfzig	73 dreiundsiebzig	96 sechsundneunzig
51 einundfünfzig	74 vierundsiebzig	97 siebenundneunzig
52 zweiundfünfzig	75 fünfundsiebzig	98 achtundneunzig
53 dreiundfünfzig	76 sechsundsiebzig	99 neunundneunzig
54 vierundfünfzig	77 siebenundsiebzig	100 hundert

Alphabet

Aa   Ää
Bb
Cc
Dd
Ee
Ff
Gg
Hh
Ii
Jj
Kk
Ll
Mm
Nn
Oo   Öö
Pp
Qq
Rr
Ss
ß
Tt
Uu   Üü
Vv
Ww
Xx
Yy
Zz

Family tree

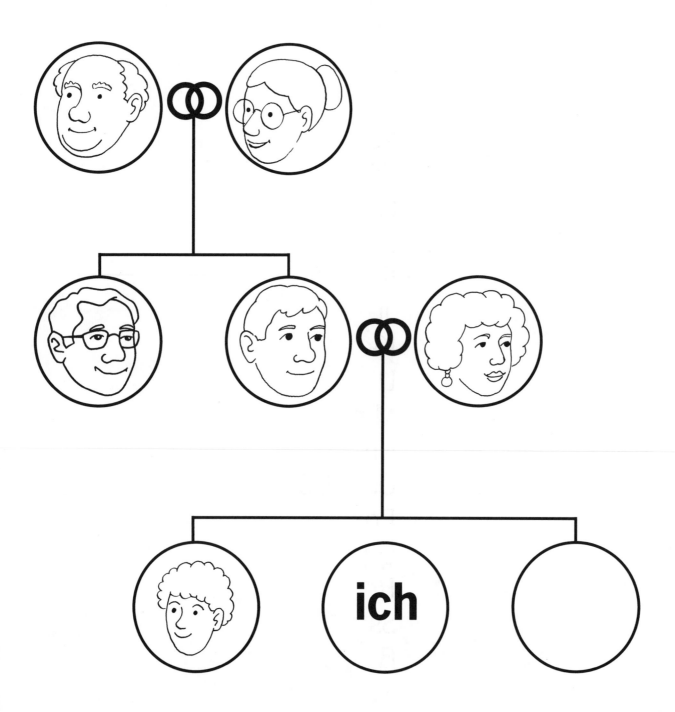

Listening/sorting

1

2

3

4

5

6

7

8

9

10

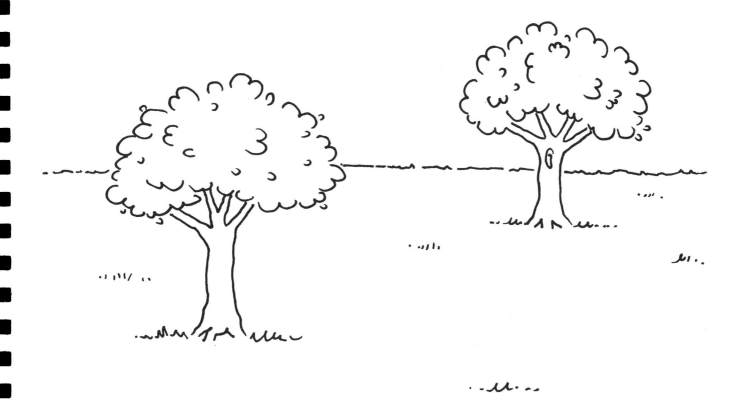

Stundenplan

Stundenplan

Montag	Dienstag	Mittwoch	Donnerstag	Freitag

Tag／Stunde	Montag	Dienstag	Mittwoch	Donnerstag	Freitag
1					
2					
3					
4					

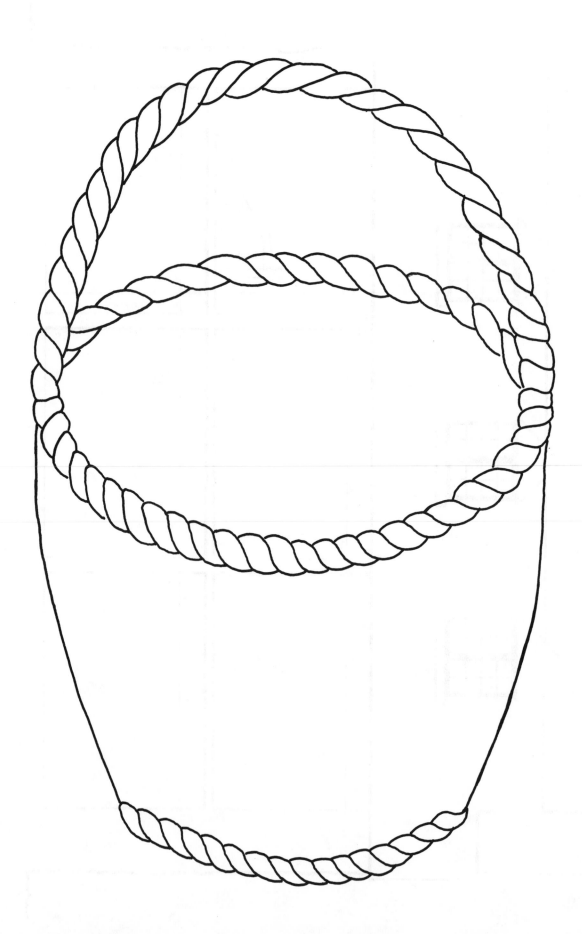

Imbiß-Stube Schnellinger

Getränke

Kleine Mahlzeiten

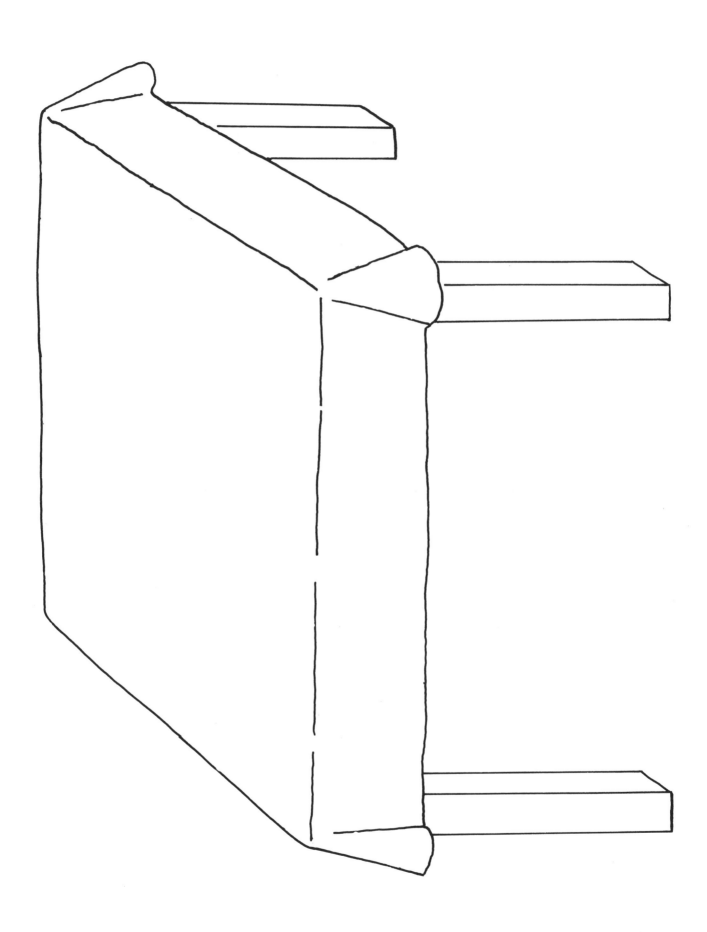

85

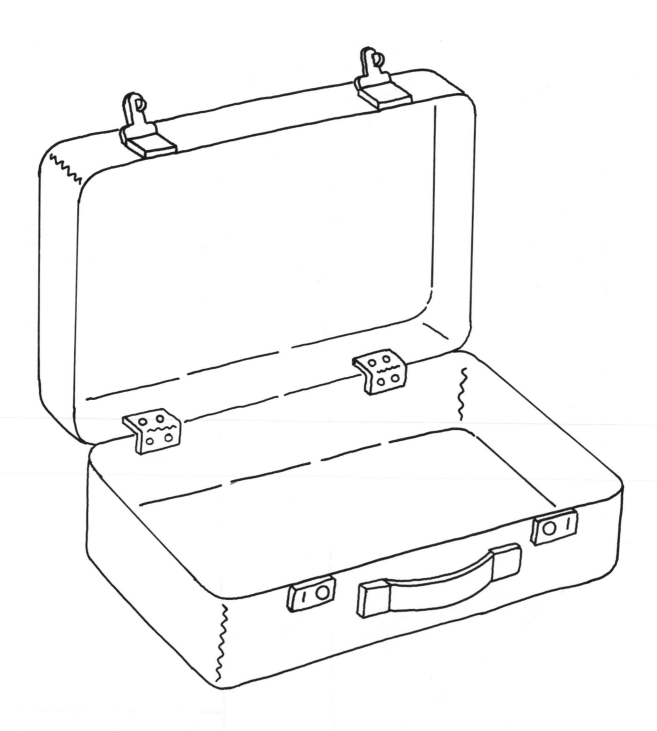

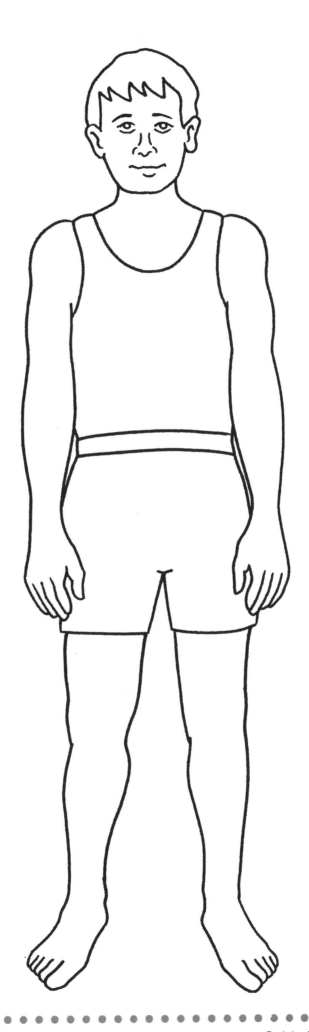

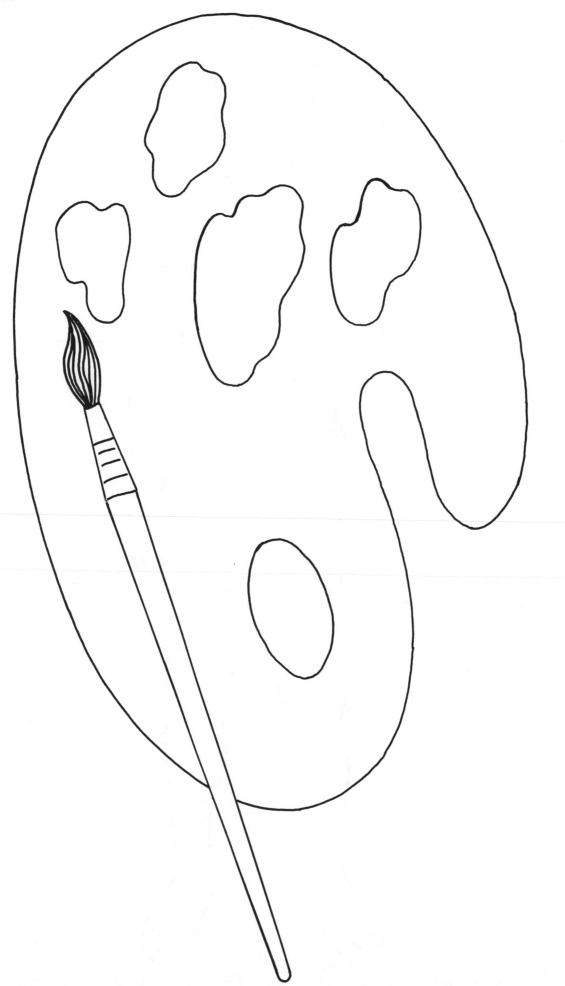

Bingo B13

MODULE 1 Here I am

Timescale
1 term

Areas of experience
A   B

Topics / Communicative objectives

Topics	Communicative objectives
(i) Greetings	Initiating and responding to simple greetings
(ii) Introducing oneself	Asking for and giving name
(iii) Classroom objects	Understanding and naming the objects in the classroom
(iv) Getting involved	Responding to instructions in the foreign language classroom
(v) Numbers and alphabet	Understanding and using numbers 0–31 and the alphabet
(vi) Personal details	Exchanging information about age and where I live

Assignments
Designing and making classroom signs

Designing and compiling a phrase book

Making ID card

Learning a short 'poem' by heart

Writing a short 'poem' or acrostic

Programme of study (part 1): Examples
1   Communicating in the target language
   (a) communicate with each other in pairs and groups and with the teacher
   (b) use language for real purposes
   (f) discuss own interests and compare them with those of others
2   Language skills
   (b) follow instructions and directions
   (d) ask and answer questions and instructions
3   Language learning skills and knowledge of language
   (a) learn by heart phrases and short extracts

Cross-curricular opportunities

Number practice	Maths
Counting and simple calculations	
Designing and making (assignments)	Design and Technology Information technology
Role play and pairwork	PSE

Opportunities for assessment

Respond to flashcards/ play games	AT1:1; AT2:1,2
Understand other people giving name	AT1:1
Ask/answer questions about name/age	AT1:1; AT2:1,2
Play *Walter sagt*	AT1:1,2
Say own name/cue card name	AT2:1
Match words to objects/pictures	AT3:1
Label pictures/objects	AT4:1

Module 1 Here I am

Topic (i) Greetings

Topic
(i) Greetings

Communicative objective
Initiating and responding to simple greetings

Linguistic objectives (examples)
Guten Tag!

Hallo + name!

Wie geht's?

Gut danke.

Und dir?

(Auch) gut.

Tschüß!

Auf Wiedersehen!

Activities
- Begin by greeting pupils and encouraging them to respond
- Reinforce meanings with flashcards
- Match words and pictures
- Pairwork – role play
- Copy-writing
- Rhyme or rap

Resources
- Greetings flashcards
- Cue cards
- Sets of pictures/cue cards for building sentences
- Template 7

- Song cassette

Few resources are needed here – these introductory lessons rely heavily on gesture, mime and role play

Assignments
Make up and perform a greetings sketch

Start to compile a phrase book

Module 1 Here I am

Topic (ii) Introducing oneself

Topic

(ii) Introducing oneself

Communicative objective

Asking for and giving name

Linguistic objectives (examples)

Wie heißt du?

Ich bin der } + name
die

Ich heiße. . . , und du?

Activities

- Simple teacher-led question and answer
- Pairs/groups as above
- Pupils take German name cards and say who they are
- Pupils take picture cards and say who they are
- Copying words and phrases
- IT opportunity

Resources

- Name cards, template 14

- Pictures of famous people (of interest to teenagers!)

Assignments

Working towards ID card and playlet

Module 1 Here I am

Topic (iii) Classroom objects

Topic
(iii) Classroom objects

Communicative objective
Understanding and naming the objects in the classroom

Linguistic objectives (examples)

das Heft (-e)	Ist das ein(e). . . ?
das Buch (¨er)	Was ist das?
das Papier	Das ist. . .
das Lineal (-e)	Ja.
der Spitzer	Nein.
das Bild (-er)	Hast du ein/einen/
das Fenster	eine. . . ?
die Tafel (-n)	Ich habe ein/einen/
die Schultasche (-n)	eine. . .
die Tür (-en)	Nein, ich habe kein/
der Tisch (-e)	keinen/keine. . .
der Stuhl (¨e)	Ich möchte. . . (bitte)
der Bleistift (-e)	Ich brauche. . .
der Kuli (-s)	Bitte (schön).
der Radiergummi (-s)	Danke (schön).
der Filzstift (-e)	Wo ist. . . ?
	Da! (and point)
	Hier! (pick up and show)

Activities
- After presentation pupils point to, touch, bring out objects
- Play *Walter sagt* with the above
- Snap and Pelmanism to match words and pictures
- True/false games
- Kim's game
- Classroom objects wordsearch
- Make up your own wordsearch
- Copy-writing to label pictures and objects
- Song

Resources
- Worksheets Set 1, 1–4
- Classroom object flashcards
- Small images to make wordsearch
- Snap and Pelmanism cards
- Bingo, template B1
- Noughts and crosses, templates 3a and 3b for OHP
- Ready-made wordsearch, template 4a or 4b
- Blank wordsearch to make up, template 4a

- Card for pupils to make labels
- Classroom objects
- Cue cards
- Song cassette

Assignments
Making classroom signs

Continuing phrase book

Module 1 Here I am

Topic (iv) Getting involved

Topic

(iv) Getting involved

Communicative objective

Responding to instructions in the foreign language classroom

Linguistic objectives (examples)

Ruhe bitte!

Aufstehen, bitte!

Setzen, bitte!

(Wir) schreiben, (bitte).

    schreiben...ab/kopieren

    lesen

    hören

    nachsprechen

    spielen

    raten

    malen

    fragen

    antworten

    gucken

    zeigen

    nehmen

Könnt ihr bitte. . . } + above verbs
Du mußt bitte. . .

Kannst du bitte. . .?

Hefte auf/zu, bitte!

Komm bitte (an die Tafel/zum Projektor)!

Wie bitte?

Lauter bitte!

Fertig!

Tschüß!

Wiedersehen!

This is a long list, but remember it is receptive rather than productive vocabulary

Activities

- After presentation use gestures and mimes to reinforce meaning
- Play *Walter sagt*
- Matching words to symbols
- Battleships
- Alphabet song/chant

Note: nothing needs to be written here

Resources

- Flashcards   classroom commands classroom objects
- Cue cards   classroom commands classroom objects
- Name cards
- Alphabet template
- Battleship template

- Classroom objects

Assignments

Making own cue cards with words and symbols to make classroom display for daily use

Module 1 Here I am

Topic (v) Numbers and alphabet

Topic
(v) Numbers and alphabet

Communicative objective
Understanding and using numbers 0–31 and the alphabet

Linguistic objectives (examples)
Numbers 0–31 (see template 15a)

Wieviele. . . ?

und dann?

Alphabet (see template 16)

Classroom objects from topic (iii)

Activities
- Counting objects
- Worksheets Set 2, 1 and 2
- Identify numbers in a sequence
- Sums
- How many times did I say?
- Matching activities
- Bingo
- Dominoes
- Singing numbers to raps/tunes
- Alphabet games – what comes next?
                          – what is missing?
- Spelling own name
- Fill in missing letter
- Crack the code

Resources
- Worksheets Set 2, 1 and 2
- Classroom object flashcards
- Song cassette
- Dominoes, template 2 for digits/words – numbers
- Number cards, template 15a

- Number cards, digits and words, for matching alphabet frieze
- Song cassette

Assignments
Alphabet/number rap

For classroom display link number cue cards in visual form with different numbers of classroom objects

Module 1 Here I am

Topic (vi) Personal details

Topic
(vi) Personal details

Communicative objective
Exchanging information about age and where I live

Linguistic objectives (examples)
Wie alt bist du?

Ich bin. . .

Wo wohnst du?

Ich wohne in. . .

Name

Vorname

Alter

Adresse

Activities
After presentation:

- Pairwork
- Simulations using mixture of name/age/town cards
- Building up sentences
- Filling out ID card
- Copy-writing of new phrases
- Worksheet Set 3, 2 can be used to practise numbers. Given words, pupils can write the digits.

Resources
- Worksheet Set 3, 2
- Name/age (number)/town cards
- Outline ID card, template 6

- Blank cassettes

Assignments
Making an ID card

Making up a dialogue and performing/recording it

Note: remember, from now on, to continue adding to the phrase book

Module 1: Here I am

General notes on the module

- This introductory module is not typical of the rest of the course.
- Its role is to introduce the pupils to the language needed to participate in later activities, to introduce the activities and games themselves, to show how mime and gesture help understanding and to get the pupils using German as quickly as possible.
- Details given in this module for the presentation of new vocabulary, etc. will not be repeated in later modules, where teaching notes will begin after the initial presentation.

1(i) Greetings

- Begin immediately by saying *Guten Tag* and shaking hands with as many pupils as possible.
- Pupils will gradually start to respond quite naturally.
- Now encourage this.
- Words and phrases should now be said to elicit all kinds of repetition by class, group and individual.
- Also encourage repetition in different ways, e.g. quietly, loudly, angrily, sadly, fast, slowly, etc. This will help to vary the very important stage of repetition, which can otherwise become boring.
- Pupils can now work in pairs/groups on greetings.
- No writing need necessarily be done at this stage, although copy-writing after a reading or aural exercise building up utterances often helps reinforcement and memory. Template 7 could be used here.

Here is a game to practise greetings.
Teacher asks pupils to leave their seats and walk around the classroom pretending they are going for a walk in the park or in town. *Bitte aufstehen! So und jetzt bitte spazierengehen!* (walk around) When teacher calls out *Stop!* [shtopp] everyone freezes for an instant waiting for the teacher's signal to release them. Pupils then turn to the nearest person and exchange handshakes and greetings. They then suddenly look at their watch pretending to have to rush off (*oh je!*) and depart in opposite directions with a *Tschüß* or *Wiedersehen!* They continue their walk until instructed once more to freeze, and so on.

Assignment

- Pupils should perform a short sketch with a small group greeting each other, shaking hands, saying *Wie geht's?* and then taking their leave.
- This greetings sketch is working towards the final dialogue of the module.
- The phrase book is important since it encourages careful copy-writing and will encourage dictionary skills later.

1(ii) Introducing oneself

- This extends Topic 1(i) by just a few phrases.
- Follow the same kind of presentation initially.
- Some pictures of famous (to today's teenagers, remember) people will add interest – pupils can choose to be somebody else or be given a person to be.

Note: we are not here introducing *Er/sie heißt* – at this stage we want nothing to confuse the giving of clear information about oneself.

- Games can be played with flashcards where the picture is only gradually revealed.
- The German name cards will serve two purposes – to introduce the pupils to German names and to give an activity similar to the one above.

Note: it is advisable to copy the names onto card, colour-coded for boys/girls, so that when pupils pick a card and pretend to be that person, they get the correct gender.

- Listening – all courses have young people greeting each other in early units, so any cassettes available to you will be useful here for pupils to recognize names and voices.

Assignment

There is no complete assignment in this small topic but pupils can add new vocabulary into their previous dialogue, and are acquiring some of the vocabulary needed for the ID card.

1(iii) Classroom objects

- This is the first set of nouns to be presented. Look carefully at the introduction to the book for suggestions of use of flashcards, worksheets and games.
- For this first wordsearch, make it simple with illustrations so that pupils learn what to do; it may be useful here to let them have a first go at making one of their own. Do **not** worry if this does not work this first time – it is practice for later.
- Encourage active participation by getting pupils to not only point to, but get up and go to touch things.
- Say you want something (*Ich möchte*) with pupils coming to give the subject to you (*Hier, bitte schön.*) again allowing movement around the class, which is vital for these pupils.
- True/false games – hold up objects/pictures saying *Ich habe ein. . .* Pupils have to decide *ja* or *nein*; this can be the whole class calling out or teams or individuals.

- Don't worry too much about endings: it's more important that the message is communicated.

Assignment
- Classroom signs prepared by the pupils will give them confidence in their writing when they see them displayed for genuine information.
- The phrase book should be continued – this can either be done under topics or alphabetically.

1(iv) Getting involved
A very simple but versatile form of command has been suggested here. The key word is emphasized; it can be used in many ways, e.g. *Bitte setzen/Könnt ihr euch bitte setzen/Kannst du dich bitte setzen*, etc. The second person singular and plural can be phased in at the teacher's discretion.
- The vocabulary in this topic relies heavily on mime and pupils can be encouraged to either mime as the teacher gives the order or to give the order as the teacher mimes.
- Pupils can then identify or guess what other pupils are miming.
- Flashcards of symbols will help with understanding, but pupils should be encouraged to think up their own symbols since they will be sure to understand these!
- Playing *Walter sagt* will reinforce understanding and gives an opportunity for movement.

Assignment
Pupils can now each make a classroom symbol with appropriate classroom language for display and daily reinforcement.

1(v) Numbers
- Present the numbers gradually throughout the whole module, 0–10, 11–20, 21–31.
- Do simple counting for sequence, counting down/backwards as well as forwards.
- Count objects in the classroom.
- Do simple activities of missing numbers or 'what comes next?' (*und dann?*).
- Introduce how to play Bingo and dominoes in class.
- Do basic mental arithmetic.
- Play battleships with numbers using template 5B.

Alphabet
- Start with the vowel sounds: a, e, i, o and u are pure sounds. Once the mouth shape is formed, don't alter it! This also applies to ä, ö and ü.
- f, l, m, n, s, ß (ss) sound virtually like their English equivalent. z almost does, but the 'tsett' hissing sound needs stressing.
- b, c, d, e, g, p, rhyme in English, and they do in German too, though the sound of 'e' will need practice.

- w rhymes with the b, c etc.
- a, h, k rhyme with each other.
- q rhymes with u.
- r say 'fresh "r"'.
- vw is what the Volkswagen is called in Germany.
- y is so strange that most pupils have no difficulty in remembering it.

Try to get a rhythm going:
   a b c d e f **g**
   h i j k l m n o **p**
   q r s t u v **w**
   x
   y
   z

- Alphabet song

The alphabet is introduced so that pupils can (a) spell important words like their name or their town, and (b) understand spellings so that they can eventually correctly record things that have only been heard, e.g. on the telephone.

The activities can echo those suggested for numbers with sequencing, tunes or raps, missing letters, etc. The name cards (template 14) could be used with letters blocked out for pupils to supply.

Crack the code: Words are written in 'code', i.e. a letter is shown as a number. Pupils should be provided with a key to help them decipher the words. For example, 7 4 3 9 6 3 5 7 = GUTEN TAG!

Pupils could also make up their own codes and produce words for others to decipher.

Assignments
- Pupils can make up their own raps or songs using numbers and letters of the alphabet.
- Pupil-produced display of numbers linked with numbers of objects reinforces concept of numbers as well as making the classroom attractive.

1(vi) Personal details
- This now completes the basic information from 1(i) and 1(ii).
- Encourage pair/group work with simple interviews.
- Name, age, town cards can be given out for pupils to build up simulated personalities.

Assignment
- Making up a dialogue and recording it is an opportunity to set up your system for pupils to record work. Not everyone will be able to do this successfully yet, but it is important practice for the rest of the course. It is usually fun anyway.
- Using template 6, pupils can now make their own ID card to be used in a real school situation, e.g. as a lunch pass, etc.

MODULE 2 Talking about people

Timescale
1 term

Areas of experience
A   B

Topics / Communicative objectives

Topics	Communicative objectives
(i) Family members	Understanding and naming members of the family
(ii) Family descriptions	Exchanging information about members of the family
(iii) Classmates	Reporting basic personal details about members of the class
(iv) Pets	Understanding and naming pets
(v) Likes and dislikes	Expressing personal opinions

Assignments
Design and make a 'wanted' poster

Scrapbook/video on family/class

Talking photo album

Likes/dislikes survey

Programme of study (part 1): Examples
1   Communicating in the target language
   (a) communicate with each other in pairs and groups and with the teacher
   (b) use language for real purposes
2   Language skills
   (a) listen attentively for gist and detail
   (h) express agreement, disagreement, personal feelings and opinions
3   Language learning skills and knowledge of language
   (a) learn by heart phrases and short extracts

Cross-curricular opportunities

Designing and making (see assignments)   Design and Technology

Surveys

Expressing opinions   }   PSE

Opportunities for assessment

Respond to flashcards	AT1:1; AT2:1
Understand names of family members	AT1:1
Understand information given to others about family	AT1:1, 2, 3
Ask/answer questions about people in family	AT1:2; AT2:1, 2
Say one or two sentences about people in family	AT2:2, 3
Draw a person from written description	AT3:1,2,3
Complete written description from picture clues	AT4:1, 2, 3

Module 2 Talking about people

Topic (i) Family members

Topic
(i) Family members

Communicative objective
Understanding and naming members of the family and giving their ages

Linguistic objectives (examples)

meine Familie

meine Mutter (Mutti)

meine Schwester/meine Schwestern

meine Großmutter (Oma)

mein Vater (Vati)

mein Bruder/meine Brüder

mein Großvater (Opa)

Das ist mein/meine. . .

Das sind meine. . .

Meine Mutter heißt. . .

Sie heißt. . .

Mein Vater heißt. . .

Er heißt. . .

Meine Schwestern heißen. . . und. . .

Sie heißen. . . und. . .

Wie alt ist dein Vater?

Er ist. . . (Jahre alt).

Wie alt ist deine Mutter?

Sie ist. . . (Jahre alt).

Wie alt sind deine Geschwister/Brüder/ Schwestern?

Sie sind. . . und. . .

Activities
- Linking family titles with flashcards and other pictures
- Naming members of picture families
- Worksheets for family
- Talking about own family
- Wordsearch
- Exchanging information about each other's families
- Numbers 1–100
- Battleships/Guessing games

Resources
- Worksheets Set 1, 1–4
- Family flashcards
- Wordsearch, template 4a or 4b
- Blank wordsearch, template 4a
- Cue cards
- Name cards
- Family tree and labels
- Battleships, template 5b

- Pupils' family photos where possible
- Cut-outs of families from magazines, or individuals to make up families
- Song cassette

Assignments
Labelled photograph or drawing of own family (simplified version); drawing and/or labelling a family tree from information given (spoken or written) can be based on famous or imaginary family (Simpsons, royal family, Addams family) with simple description written from 'child's' perspective, e.g. *Ich heiße Bart Simpson. Meine Mutter heißt Marge und sie ist 45.*

Module 2 Talking about people

Topic (ii) Family descriptions

Topic
(ii) Family descriptions

Communicative objective
Exchanging information about members of the family

Linguistic objectives (examples)

Wie ist dein/deine. . . ?

Wie ist (+ name)*?*

Er ist. . .

Sie ist. . .

groß

mittelgroß

klein

schlank

vollschlank

dick

. . .und er/sie ist. . .

nett

lustig

frech

doof

sehr

sehr, sehr

Activities
- Talking about age of brothers/sisters
- Describing people from pictures/photos
- Worksheets linking descriptions with people
- Describing own family members
- Exchanging information about families
- Repetition 'chain'
- Talking about someone's personality
- Giving opinions

Resources
- Worksheets Set 2, 1 and 2
- Description flashcards
- Cue cards
- Number cards

- Magazine pictures/cartoons of different-sized people
- Song cassette

Assignments
Scrapbook on family or talking photo album

DEUTSCH? KEIN PROBLEM!

Module 2 Talking about people

Topic (iii) Classmates

Topic
(iii) Classmates

Communicative objective
Reporting basic personal details about members of the class

Linguistic objectives (examples)

Wie heißt dein (bester) Freund?

Wie heißt deine (beste) Freundin?

Wie heißt dein Nachbar?

Wie heißt deine Nachbarin?

Er/sie heißt. . .

Wie alt ist er/sie?

Er/sie ist. . . (Jahre alt).

Wie ist er/sie?

Er/sie ist groß/klein, etc.

Er/sie hat	*lange*	*Haare.*
	mittellange	
	kurze	
	wellige	
	lockige	
	glatte	
	blonde	
	braune	
	schwarze	
	rote	
	blaue	*Augen.*
	grüne	
	braune	
	graue	

Activities
• Build on 2(ii) for initial descriptions

• Revise Numbers for giving ages

• Worksheets about descriptions

• Drawing and colouring from information given (spoken or written)

• Completing a spoken or written description from visual clues

• Describing people in the class

• Guessing game from teacher's then pupils' descriptions

• Pairwork – information gap

Resources
• Worksheets Set 2, 1 and 2

• Worksheet Set 3, 3 for listening (see Teaching notes page 104)

• Description flashcards

• Made-up wordsearch, template 4a or 4b

• Blank wordsearch, template 4a

• Picture/name/age (number) cards for sentence building

• Colour cards

• Large felt tips or colouring pens

• Pictures of heads showing different hair styles/colours

• Song cassette

Assignments
'Wanted' poster of real or imaginary person

Module 2 Talking about people

Topic (iv) Pets

Topic
(iv) Pets

Communicative objective
Understanding, naming and describing pets

Giving basic opinions or reactions

Linguistic objectives (examples)

Hast du. . . ?

Ich habe	*einen Vogel/zwei Vögel.*
	einen Goldfisch/zwei Goldfische.
	einen Hamster/zwei Hamster.
	einen Hund/zwei Hunde.
	eine Katze/zwei Katzen.
	eine Schildkröte/zwei Schildkröten.
	eine Maus/zwei Mäuse.
	eine Springmaus/zwei Springmäuse.
	ein Kaninchen/zwei Kaninchen.
	ein Pferd/Pony/zwei Pferde/Ponys.

Er/sie ist ⎫ *süß.*
Sie sind ⎭ *lustig.*
      frech.
      doof.
      gefährlich.
      eklig.

Activities

- Flashcard guessing games
- All games as suggested in Introduction
- Worksheets Set 1, 1–4, Set 3, 1–2
- Wordsearch and making a wordsearch
- Drawing and labelling
- Questions and answers
- Song/rhyme
- Revision of numbers

Resources

- Worksheets Set 1, 1–4, Set 3, 1–2
- Animal flashcards
- Pelmanism/snap cards, template 1
- Beetle, template 1
- Dominoes, template 2
- Bingo, template B2
- Made-up wordsearch, template 4a or 4b
- Blank wordsearch, template 4a
- Survey sheet, template 10

- Song cassette

Assignments

Class display of labelled pictures (drawn or cut out) of pets

Designing or completing a 'word comb'

Poster of own or imagined pet with description

Designing a small ad (with or without picture) for lost pet or pet for sale

Module 2 Talking about people

Topic (v) Likes and dislikes

Topic
(v) Likes and dislikes

Communicative objective
Expressing personal opinions

Linguistic objectives (examples)

Magst du	*Pferde?*
	Hunde?
	Fische?
	Mäuse?
	Hamster?
	Kaninchen?
	Vögel?
	Springmäuse?
	Katzen?
	Schildkröten?

Ja, ich liebe. . .

Ja, ich mag. . .

Nein, ich mag keine. . .

Nein, ich hasse. . .

Nein, ich mag lieber. . .

Ja, sehr gern.

Nein, nicht so gern.

Activities
- Linking likes and dislikes to pets
- Worksheets Set 2, 1–3
- Pelmanism and snap with likes/dislikes
- Record pupil preferences of animals on likes/dislikes sheets (Set 2, 4)
- Listening exercise

Resources
- Worksheets Set 1 (any)
- Animal flashcards
- Likes/dislikes flashcards
- Worksheets Set 2, 1–4
- Likes/dislikes profile, template 9
- Survey sheet, template 10

- Song cassette

Assignments
Class survey of likes/dislikes and pets; graph/pie chart

Module 2: Talking about people

2(i) Family members

Note: although possessive pronouns come into this topic, there is no need, at this stage, for these to be taken as a teaching point. As only some pupils will manage such grammatical details, remember that effective communication is the aim.

- The best initial presentation for family members would be the teacher's own family with photographs.
- The flashcard family should be presented as just **a** family so that it can be linked by pupils with *mein/meine*, etc.
- Pictures of families could have one of the children circled as the spokesperson for naming the family, (we do not want to introduce *sein/seine*, etc. here).
- Worksheets Set 1, 1–4 and a made-up wordsearch can reinforce words.
- From photographs or drawings pupils can introduce/answer questions about their own family.
- Pupils can then exchange information about families.

Note: if *er/sie* is a problem, the pupil can simply say *Meine Mutter heißt. . .*, etc. Introduce numbers 30–100. To help pupils cope with the idea of saying the numbers 'back-to-front' (e.g. *zweiundvierzig*, 42) they can play Battleships (template 5b) with the numbers 20, 30, 40 etc. going across and the single digits going down.

Assignment

Pupils may now label a photograph of their own family if one is available or draw their family – *Hier ist mein Vater; das ist meine Mutter*, etc. and/or draw and label a family tree.

2(ii) Family descriptions

- After introduction of descriptions link these with pictures from magazines or cartoons.
- Worksheets Set 2, 1 and 2 will then link family member with description. You may prefer to leave sheet 3 at present because it is a more complicated exercise and these are early days in the learning process.
- Repetition 'chain' – to add variety to repetition, have pictures or OHTs, to make simple description, e.g. *Meine Mutter ist groß*, and change either the person or the description – *Meine Mutter ist klein* or *Mein Vater ist groß*. This can be speeded up with sections of the class taking it in turns to respond.

- Pupils will then describe their own family using photographs and drawings.
- Pairwork – exchanging information about family members.

Note: Many children have rather complicated families and some feel more comfortable describing a given or imaginary family rather than their own. Others like to create a family for themselves using pictures of people cut out from magazines.

Assignment

Pupils can build up a family scrapbook with photographs or drawings of family members and family activities, etc. **or** they can record onto cassette a presentation of their family, to link with a photo or drawing.

2(iii) Classmates

Note: this topic builds on 2(ii) with added detail, which may then be used to describe the family in more detail, but this is at the discretion of the teacher (pupils need variety, so this could be seen as too much of the same).

- After the initial presentation of new words, worksheets Set 2, 1 and 2 can link names and any kind of descriptive detail to encourage spoken or written sentences.
- Use worksheet Set 3, 3 for a listening activity. Pupils tick who is being described.
- Playing cards of nouns, ages and other descriptive details can then be used as a stimulus for lengthier spoken or written descriptions, or revision of numbers.
- 'Colour cards' can be made simply by cutting up card of different colours and writing the colour names on them.
  Sets of large felt-tip pens for colouring are useful for introducing colours. Pens can be used for listening and pointing/touching or listening and sorting activities, chain games and memory games.
  Note: It is often better to teach the colours first on their own without endings. This tends to prevent pupils from using the declined forms of the adjectives wrongly later; it also makes it easier for them to recognize them in different contexts.
- Teachers can give descriptive information for pupils to draw or colour from.
- Pairwork – information gap: pupils each draw a person and give information to each other to complete a second drawing and then compare pictures.

Assignment

Pupils can make up 'wanted' posters with a drawing and a description below. Encourage them to use other information such as name and nickname (*Spitzname*). If real people are chosen, e.g. teachers/famous people, etc. the sheets can be put around the room and form the source of a guessing game, i.e. **names** are not included on the poster.

2(iv) Pets

- This topic lends itself well to most of the games, so it is an excellent opportunity to teach the games themselves as well as the linguistic objectives.
- Using playing cards of animals, question and answer activities can be set up, e.g. cards face down on the table, one pupil picks one up, the other has to guess what it is: *Hast du einen Hamster? Nein. Hast du eine Maus? Ja.* Then the other pupil has a turn. This can be scored but does not have to be.
- Numbers can be revised again by asking/giving pets' ages.
- The survey sheet, template 10, is suggested here as a trial run of how to do a survey ready for 2(v). This time it is suggested that pupils' names/animals are ticked to find out who (or how many) has what.

Assignment

Pupils draw or cut out animals and label them for an animal frieze or 'garden' of animals on Bingo template B2.

Pupils write a very simple, small advertisement for the 'Lost and found' column or the 'Pets' (*Tiermarkt*) column in the local paper. Alternatively, they could write a message to be put up in a newsagent's window about a pet for sale (*zu verkaufen*) or gone missing (*verloren*) or found (*gefunden*). They may simply draw the pet, having read a small ad (written by the teacher or another pupil). Create a noticeboard with the messages/adverts.

2(v) Likes and dislikes

- The heart symbols can be presented, repeated and reinforced with basic worksheets.
- Then link likes/dislikes with animals using pictures (board or OHT) and do Worksheets Set 2, 1–2, also 3 if pupils are ready for gap-filling.
- Elicit information from pupils. Then encourage pupils to exchange information.
- Pelmanism can be played as a stimulus for sentence-building based on pictures.
- The personal profile likes/dislikes sheet, template 9, can be started – the idea is that, if they are enlarged to A3, pupils can gradually add more details as further topics are completed.
- Pupils can have to listen for either **who** likes what or **what** is liked or disliked. Worksheets Set 2, 4 and Set 3, 3 (see introduction to worksheets).

Assignment

The suggested survey will plot animals against heart symbols to get numbers of pupils who like/dislike, etc. certain animals. This information may then be represented in the form of a bar graph.

MODULE 3 My school

Timescale
1 term

Areas of experience
A

Topics / Communicative objectives

Topics	Communicative objectives
(i) Subjects	Understanding and naming school subjects
(ii) Likes and dislikes	Exchanging opinions about school subjects
(iii) Days of the week	Describing and expressing opinions about days at school
(iv) The timetable	Exchanging information about the daily timetable
(v) Rooms in school	Understanding and naming the main points in the school and giving directions

Assignments
Labels for rooms in school/school subjects

Class survey/graph

Make up own school timetable

School plan (show visitor round)

Programme of study (part 1): Examples
1 Communicating in the target language
  (a) communicate with each other in pairs and groups and with the teacher
  (b) use language for real purposes
  (c) develop understanding and skills through a range of language activities
  (f) discuss own interests and compare them with those of others
2 Language skills
  (a) listen attentively for gist and detail
  (b) follow instructions and directions
  (h) express agreement, disagreement, personal feelings and opinions
3 Language learning skills and knowledge of language
  (a) learn by heart phrases and short extracts

Cross-curricular opportunities

Number practice	Mathematics
Graphs	
Display design	Technology
School lay-out plan	

Opportunities for assessment

Respond to flashcards/play games	AT1:1; AT2:1
Understand names of subjects or rooms	AT1:1
Understand other people's opinions about subjects	AT1:2
Ask/answer survey questions	AT1:2; AT2:1,2,3
Understand a simple timetable	AT3:1
Complete a wordsearch	AT3:1
Label pictures about school	AT4:1
Write own timetable	AT4:1,2
Write a few sentences about school	AT4:3
Fill in a timetable or school layout plan from information (spoken or written)	AT1:2 AT2:1,2,3 AT3:2 AT4:2

Module 3 My school

Topic (i) Subjects

Topic
(i) Subjects

Communicative objective
Understanding and naming school subjects

Linguistic objectives (examples)

Englisch

Mathe

Deutsch

Französisch

Naturwissenschaften (Biologie/Chemie/Physik)

Geschichte

Erdkunde

Religion

Musik

Sport

Technik/Werken

Kunst

Theater

Informatik

Welche Fächer hast du?

Ich habe. . .

- Teachers should choose those subjects appropriate to their pupils.

Activities
- Flashcard presentation
- Matching word and symbol
- Matching/memory games
- Worksheets Set 1, 1–4
- Wordsearch and making a wordsearch
- Drawing and labelling for display
- Play Bingo level 1, template B3
- Play dominoes, template 2

Resources
- Worksheets Set 1, 1–4
- Subject flashcards
- Variety of games from dominoes, template 2 snap/Pelmanism, template 1
- Made-up wordsearch, template 4b
- Blank wordsearch, template 4a
- Bingo level 1, template B3
- Cue cards

- Song cassette

Assignments
Labelled pictures of school subjects for classroom display

Module 3 My school

Topic (ii) Likes and dislikes

Topic
(ii) Likes and dislikes

Communicative objective
Exchanging opinions about school subjects

Linguistic objectives (examples)

Magst du (gern). . . ?

Ja, ich liebe. . .

Ja, ich mag. . .

Nein, ich mag. . . nicht.

Ja, ich mag. . . sehr gern.

Nein, ich mag. . . nicht (so) gern.

Nein, ich hasse. . .

Was magst du (gern)?

Ich mag (gern). . .

Warum?

Es ist toll.

Deutsch ist   interessant.

leicht/einfach.

doof/schrecklich.

langweilig.

schwierig.

Magst du lieber Mathe oder Englisch? Ich mag lieber. . .

Was ist dein Lieblingsfach?

Mein Lieblingsfach ist. . .

Ich liebe. . .

Wieviele Schüler. . . ?

Activities
- Flashcard presentation
- Question and answer – class
- Worksheets Set 2, 1–4
  – making sentences
  – listen and draw
  – gap-filling
- Writing about likes/dislikes from profile, template 9
- Class survey with oral/written follow-up
- Pairwork } oral
  Groupwork

Resources
- Worksheets Set 2, 1–3
- Subject flashcards
- Likes/dislikes flashcards
- Snap cards for matching/making up sentences
- Survey sheet, template 10
- Likes/dislikes profile, template 9

- Song cassette

Assignments
Class survey

Module 3 My school

Topic (iii) Days of the week

Topic
(iii) Days of the week

Communicative objective
Expressing opinions about days at school

Linguistic objectives (examples)

Days of the week (see templates 13a and 13b)

Was hast du am Montag?	*Ich habe. . . und. . . und. . . Am Montag habe ich (zuerst). . . und (dann). . .*
Magst du Dienstag?	*Nein, Dienstag ist doof/ schrecklich. Nein, ich hasse Dienstag.*
Warum?	*Ich habe. . . und. . .*
Was ist dein Lieblingstag?	*(Mein Lieblingstag ist) Montag.*
Warum?	*Ich habe Deutsch (und. . .) und dann. . .*
Welcher Tag. . . ?	

Activities

- Flashcard presentation
- Linked presentation days and subjects
- Matching games/activities
- Days of the week rap
- Pairwork – sequencing days
- Pairwork – making up words from syllables
- Copy-writing
- Questions and answers about opinions
- Building picture sentences
- Pairwork – describing and identifying days on the timetable
- Play Battleships (days/subjects), template 5b

Resources

- Subject flashcards
- Likes and dislikes flashcards
- Days of the week cue cards, templates 13a and 13b
- Cut-up day cards for re-arranging syllables. (See Teaching notes page 112.)
- Snap cards, template 1
- Made-up wordsearch, template 4a or 4b
- Battleships, blank template 5b

- Song cassette

Assignments
Working towards a timetable

Module 3 My school

Topic (iv) The timetable

Topic
(iv) The timetable

Communicative objective
Exchanging information about the daily timetable

Linguistic objectives (examples)
days of the week

numbers 1–10

opinions vocabulary

der Stundenplan

in der ersten Stunde

in der zweiten Stunde

in der dritten Stunde

in der vierten Stunde

in der fünften Stunde

in der sechsten Stunde

in der letzten Stunde

die Stunde

die Doppelstunde

um 9(Uhr)/10(Uhr) etc.

vor

nach

Vor/nach der Pause

die Pause

die Mittagspause

(Dienstag) vormittags/nachmittags

(zu)erst Mathe

dann Deutsch e.g. *Ich habe (zu)erst Mathe und dann Deutsch*

Was hast du Montag in der ersten Stunde? – Englisch.

Activities
- OHP/board – large timetable to fill in
- Questions and answers
- Bingo with days and subjects
- Oral and written work, worksheets Set 2
- Daily timetable
- Pairwork – information gap activity completing gaps on a partially filled in timetable

Resources
- Flashcards subjects
       timetable
- Worksheets Set 2
- Day cards
- Bingo timetable, templates B3 and B4

- Song cassette

Assignments
Make up own school timetable

Module 3 My school

Topic (v) Rooms in school

Topic
(v) Rooms in school

Communicative objective
Understanding and naming the main points in the school and giving directions

Linguistic objectives (examples)

die Bücherei/die Bibliothek

das Sekretariat/das Schulbüro

die Kantine

die Schule

der Gang/der Korridor

der Schulhof

die Turnhalle/die Sporthalle

der Chemiesaal (pl. Chemiesäle)

der Biologiesaal

der Physiksaal

die Rezeption/die Anmeldung

das Klassenzimmer/der Klassensaal

der Sportplatz

(hier) geradeaus

(hier) rechts

(da) links

Hier ist. . .

Da ist. . .

Hier sind die. . .

Gehen Sie. . ./Geh. . . !

Activities
- Rooms in school flashcards, then combine with directions
- Snap and Pelmanism matching words and pictures
- Worksheets Set 1, 1–4
- Worksheet Set 2, 1–2 linking position and places in school
- Wordsearch and making a wordsearch
- Follow spoken directions referring to plan on OHP
- Follow directions in school corridors, etc.

Resources
- Worksheets Set 1, 1–4
- Worksheets Set 2, 1–2
- School flashcards
- Pelmanism/snap, template 1
- Made-up wordsearch, template 4b
- Blank wordsearch, template 4a
- Cue cards

- Simple plan of school on OHP

Assignments
Making up a plan of the school

Showing someone around the school

Module 3: My school

3(i) Subjects
See introduction for all suggested activities.

Assignment
Pupils draw symbols for school subjects and label them for display.

3(ii) Likes and dislikes
- Link these flashcards with subjects to elicit: *Ich mag (Sport)*.
- Two cards presented to individuals to elicit similar sentence: *Ich mag Sport und Deutsch*.
- Pupil picks two cards and shows them to class. Teacher: *Magst du. . . ?* Pupil answers according to cards in hand *Ja, ich mag* or *Nein, ich hasse. . .*
- Using small-sized cards pupils make up own picture sentences showing personal likes and dislikes. These can be the basis for oral or written work as well as pair/group question and answer work.

Preference
This should be introduced at the discretion of the teacher. Many pupils find it difficult to distinguish between *ich liebe* and *ich mag lieber*. It might be easier just to concentrate on the favourite subject *mein Lieblingsfach*, rather than to ask which of two subjects they prefer.
- Use *mögen* + subject flashcards.
  Question: *Magst du lieber. . . oder. . . ?*
  Teacher shows pupils two subject cards and invites them to take the card which shows the preferred subject. *Ich mag lieber. . .*
- Pupils can then be given two subject cards and answer questions referring to them, holding up their preference.

Opinions
- Presentation of pairs of flashcards to elicit *Deutsch ist toll*, etc.
- Pupil fixes pairs of cards on board for class to describe.
- Similar work in pairs/groups with smaller cards, leading to oral or written work.

Linking likes and dislikes to opinions
- Use the three sets of flashcards to build up picture sentences for oral and/or written work, e.g. subject, preference, opinion.
- Smaller cards can be given out to pupils to make picture sentences describing their own opinions, e.g. *Ich mag Erdkunde, es ist interessant*, etc.

Assignment
- To do survey, use blank sheet – pupils plot names against subjects and put like/dislike symbol in the squares.
- Use the completed survey for oral work, e.g. *Wer mag. . . ? Wieviele Schüler mögen. . . ?*

3(iii) Days of the week
- Present days of the week with word cue cards.
- Activities from the front for pupils to practise sequencing these.
- Sets of day cards to pairs/groups to do the same.
- These could then be carefully copied.
- Large cue cards cut up into halves/syllables for pupils to rebuild words – at front of class. Cut *Mo/ntag* not *Mon/tag*, etc. or too many combinations will be correct.
- Smaller sets of above for pair/group work.
- Wordsearch.
- Play Battleships putting days against subjects on the grid.

Describing a day on the timetable
- Link days with subjects, just as lists under days at this stage.
- Pupils come out and build up their lists for different days.
- Use a simple timetable with subjects represented in pictures or words. Give a short sequence of subjects from a particular day and ask pupils to name the day, e.g. *Ich habe zuerst Mathe, dann Deutsch und dann Sport. Welcher Tag ist das?* Pupils can then do the same in pairs.
- Pupils describe a whole day using *zuerst. . . und dann. . .*

Assignment
Pupils can begin to build up their timetable ready for Topic (iv).
Pupils describe their favourite day including one or two comments/opinions. *Ich habe zuerst Sport, das ist toll; dann Mathe, das ist interessant*, etc.

3(iv) The timetable
- On a large blank timetable fill in days and lesson numbers (time need not be introduced).
- At this stage vocabulary for break, lunch, morning, afternoon, before and after can be introduced at the teacher's discretion.
- Play Bingo levels 2 and 3. Level 2 – lessons are put on particular days so the day and the lesson need

to be as the teacher calls them out; Level 3 can be further complicated by lessons being inserted in particular slots on particular days.

- Give pupils individual blank timetables to fill in with pictures/words.
- Questions and answers about where lessons are on the timetable.

Assignment
On the blank timetable (Bingo template B5) pupils can draw or write in their own or an ideal timetable. Teachers may need to supply their own blank if their school timetable differs from the one supplied.

3(v) Rooms in school
See introduction for all suggested activities.

Directions
- Picture/cue cards around class for pupils to direct each other.
- Simple plan of school on board/OHP as stimulus for listening/oral/written work.
- Worksheets Set 2 will link position/direction and room.

Assignment
If the school plan is complex, provide a clear outline for pupils. To show someone around, indicate rooms with *Hier ist. . .* or *Da ist. . .* + name of room.

MODULE 4 Where we live

Timescale

1 term

Areas of experience

A C

Topics / **Communicative objectives**

(i) Location — Exchanging information about where the home is

(ii) Homes — Exchanging information about types of home

(iii) Rooms — Understanding and naming the rooms in the house

(iv) Directions — Understanding and saying where rooms are in the house

(v) Furniture — Understanding and naming articles of furniture

(vi) Inside the home — Exchanging detailed information about the home

Assignments

Scrapbook

Design a house

Design and make estate agent's poster/circular

Interview other people about their home (audio or video)

Programme of study (part 1): Examples

1 Communicating in the target language
   - (a) communicate with each other in pairs and groups and with the teacher
   - (c) develop understanding and skills through a range of language activities
2 Language skills
   - (b) follow instructions and directions
   - (k) copy words, phrases and sentences
4 Cultural awareness
   - (a) work with authentic materials

Cross-curricular opportunities

Designing and making	Design and Technology
Understanding that different people have different homes	PSE

Opportunities for assessment

Respond to flashcards	AT1:1; AT2:1
Understand names of rooms/furniture	AT1:1
Understand where rooms are in house	AT1:2,3
Ask/answer questions about where people live	AT1:2; AT2:1,2
Say/record a few sentences about ideal house	AT2:2,3
Match room/furniture words with pictures	AT3:1
Draw house/room from written description	AT3:1,2,3
Label rooms in house	AT4:1
Write a few sentences about ideal house	AT4:3

DEUTSCH? KEIN PROBLEM!

Module 4 Where we live

Topic (i) Location

Topic
(i) Location

Communicative objective
Exchanging information about where the home is

Linguistic objectives (examples)

Wo wohnst du?

Ich wohne in (Southampton) in England.

Ich wohne in Schottland.

       Großbritannien.

Wo wohnt Jens?

      Herr Neumann?

      Frau Neumann?

      die Familie Neumann?

      er?

      sie?

Er/sie wohnt in Frankfurt in Deutschland.

Ich wohne in der Stadt.

      in einem Dorf.

      auf dem Land.

      an der Küste.

      in der Nähe von [town].

Activities
- Flashcard/cue card presentation
- Pairwork – role play/information gap
- Matching word/picture
- Making sentences
- Matching/making speech bubbles with stimulus pictures

Resources
- Flashcards – as linguistic objectives
- Made-up wordsearch, template 4b, with German towns, template 17
- Blank speech bubbles, template 7
- Town cue cards

- Sentence cards cut up for re-making
- Magazines and realia (copies) to cut up

Assignments
Working towards collage of display work
(Topic (ii))

Module 4 Where we live

Topic (ii) Homes

Topic

(ii) Homes

Communicative objective

Exchanging information about types of home

Linguistic objectives (examples)

das Haus

die Wohnung

die Garage

der Garten

der Balkon

Wie wohnst du?

Wir haben ein (kleines) Haus.

Ich habe eine (große) Wohnung.

          eine Dreizimmerwohnung.

mit Garten

mit Garage

mit Balkon

Ist das Haus mit. . . ?

Und wie wohnt Jens?

Jens hat ein Haus/eine Wohnung.

Er/sie hat. . .

Activities

- Flashcard presentation
- Questions and answers about selves
- Questions about others (class and flashcard)
- Pairwork – simulation
- Drawing and labelling
- Worksheets Set 2, 1–3. Use two details in each case from people/town/country/type of dwelling/area
- Making sentences
- Collage and captions

Resources

- House flashcards
- Cue cards
- German name cue cards, template 14
- Worksheets Set 2, 1–3

- Magazines for cutting up
- Realia from Germany; you can **send** for:
  – leaflets showing houses from *Immobilienmakler*
  – newspapers for adverts
  – pictures of German houses
- Song cassette

Assignments

Working towards collage and caption display work

Module 4 Where we live

Topic (iii) Rooms

Topic
(iii) Rooms

Communicative objective
Understanding and naming the rooms in the house

Linguistic objectives (examples)
Kannst du dein Haus/deine Wohnung beschreiben?

die Küche

die Toilette

das Zimmer
(mein Zimmer = my room/my bedroom)

das Wohnzimmer

das Eßzimmer

das Schlafzimmer (= master bedroom)

das Bad(ezimmer)

die Treppe

die Terrasse

Das Haus/Die Wohnung hat. . .

Es gibt. . .

Zu verkaufen

Zu vermieten

Activities
- Flashcard presentation
- Worksheets matching words/pictures
- Pupils build up house on OHT
- Questions and answers about own house
- Pairwork – getting information/information gap simulation
- Speaking/writing about own home
- IT opportunity

Resources
- Worksheets Set 1, 1–4
- Rooms flashcards
- Bingo, template B6
- Beetle, template 1 (sets of rooms)
- Made-up wordsearch
- OHT house and furniture
- Cue cards

- German magazines for illustrations
- Song cassette

Assignments
Design an ideal house/flat/holiday cottage

Estate agent's poster of house for sale

Module 4 Where we live

Topic (iv) Directions

Topic
(iv) Directions

Communicative objective
Understanding and saying where rooms are in the house

Linguistic objectives (examples)

Wo ist. . . ?

Wo sind. . . ?

rechts (von)

links (von)

unten/im Erdgeschoß

oben/im ersten Stock

neben

gegenüber

Activities
- Flashcard presentation of 'position' words
- Practice:
  – using true/false
  – teacher describes, pupils come out and match pictures (OHP or board)
- Pupils complete plan from instructions (spoken/written)
- Worksheets Set 2, 1–2

Resources
- Flashcards showing pairs of rooms
- Worksheets Set 2, 1–2
- Bingo, template B6
- Prepared commentary (teacher) of position of rooms in houses for listening practice
- Sentence cards for matching with pictures

- Song cassette

Assignments
Recorded commentary to show a visitor around the already designed ideal home or own home

Module 4 Where we live

Topic (v) Furniture

Topic
(v) Furniture

Communicative objective
Understanding and naming articles of furniture

Linguistic objectives (examples)
der Schrank (¨e)

der Kleiderschrank (¨e)

das Sofa (-s)

der Sessel (-)

der Tisch (-e)

der Stuhl (¨e)

der Teppich (-e)

die HIFI-Anlage (-n)

das Bett (-en)

der Fernseher (-)

die Lampe (-n)

die Gardinen (pl)

die Kommode (-n)

die Dusche (-n)

Die Badewanne

prepositions from Topic (iv)

Activities
- Flashcard presentation
- Worksheets for recognition
- Matching games
- Bingo levels 1–3
- Wordsearch
- Building up rooms – OHT/pictures/cut-outs teacher-led then pairwork
- Noughts and crosses
- Memory games
- Make an inventory list of a hotel room

Resources
- Worksheets Set 1, 1–4, Set 3, 1–2
- Furniture flashcards
- Snap/Pelmanism, template 1
- Beetle, template 1
- Bingo, template B6
- Made-up wordsearch, template 4a or 4b
- Noughts and crosses, template 3a and 3b
- OHT pictures of rooms
- Furniture cue cards

- Magazines and catalogues for cutting up
- IT opportunity (*Umziehen*; *Meine Welt*)
- Song cassette

Assignments
Design a room, draw it or make a collage, labelled

Module 4 Where we live

Topic (vi) Inside the home

Topic

(vi) Inside the home

Communicative objective

Exchanging detailed information about the home

Linguistic objectives (examples)

Wo ist. . . ?

Wo sind die. . . ?

Was gibt es im Wohnzimmer/in der Küche?

rooms see Topic (iii)

furniture see Topic (v)

colours from 2(iii)

weiß

gelb

rosa*

lila*

Welche Farbe hat. . . ?

Welche Farbe haben die. . . ?

*lila and *rosa* are invariable adjectives

Activities

- Matching furniture to rooms:
  – flashcards
  – OHTs
  – Worksheets Set 2 using the double-box to link furniture with room

- Teacher-led then pairwork questions and answers about ideal room (previous assignment) or rooms of own home

Resources

- Worksheets Set 2, 1–3

- All module 4 flashcards

- Bingo, template B6

- Beetle, template 1, rooms or furniture

- All module 4 cue cards

- Magazine or catalogue pictures of rooms

- Song cassette

Assignments

Recorded or written description of own room/any room of own home (illustrated) or of ideal room (previous assignment)

Module 4: Where we live

Resources for the whole module

Pictures of old and modern German houses would be useful – possible sources:
- German magazines
- Photographs
- House sale adverts from newspapers or from *Immobilienmakler* offices

Also, plenty of English magazines and mail order or store catalogues with pictures of rooms and furniture for assignments and general illustration. All illustrations for this module can either be cut out from magazines, or made from the visuals supplied, or drawn.

Games for the whole module

Bingo level 1 – furniture, one item in any room AT1:1
2 – furniture in a particular room AT1:2
3 – more than one item in each room
Beetle – collect either rooms to complete house, or furniture to complete room(s).

4(i) Location

- Presentation of the new vocabulary is no real problem because the vocabulary is so limited in this topic.
- The use of *Er/sie wohnt* as well as *Ich wohne* will need a lot of practice in a variety of ways. For this, names of pupils can be used, or German name cards given out, or name cards linked with pictures of people cut out from magazines.
- Spoken/written accounts can be built up using pictures of people, name cue cards, town cue cards (use the blank town sign picture master to create these), location vocabulary, e.g. *Herr Schmidt wohnt in Lauenburg. Das ist in (Nord)Deutschland, in der Nähe von Hamburg.*
- Groups/pairs of pupils could build up the picture sentence and then either match it to phrase cards or write their own sentences (practice for the assignment).

Assignment
Pupils can start to write sentences to match pictures ready for 4(ii).

4(ii) Homes

- This topic builds on the previous one, adding more information, including type and size of the home.
- As in 4(i) picture sentences can be made, this time including the type of accommodation.

- The worksheets allow a variety of linked information to be used to build sentences, or for gap-filling (Set 2, sheet 3).
- The pairwork can be a simulation or a gap-filling exercise, with pupils given complete or incomplete information about imaginary people to exchange.
- Speech bubbles could then be matched to illustrations of such information.
- And finally, speech bubbles could be written by pupils for the above.

Assignment
The pupils now build up their own collage with appropriate speech bubbles. This could be individual, pair or group work.

4(iii) Rooms

- Present new vocabulary by using flashcards and by using Worksheets Set 1, 1–4.
- Using the board and flashcards or OHP, pupils can follow instructions: *Wo ist die Küche? Zeig mir* (show me) *die Küche*, etc. This could be made more challenging by using a ground plan with symbols, rather than pictures, to show rooms.
- Pupils can then list the rooms seen in the house/flat. *Die Wohnung hat. . .* or *Es gibt. . .*
- At this stage numbers can also be added. Beetle could now be played to build up a house.
- Question and answer work about rooms in their own homes is now appropriate, followed by pairwork, e.g. information gap or interviewing one another.

Assignment
The assignment simply allows creative use of the newly acquired vocabulary, encouraging labelling and simple description. (Remember, all written work can be alternatively spoken and recorded.)

4(iv) Directions

- A simple outline for 'upstairs/downstairs' will initially place rooms.
- Using pairs of pictures, *rechts/links* can be introduced.
- Using three or more pictures *neben* can be introduced. Use plenty of structured substitution drills to help with the dative, e.g. *neben dem Bad, neben dem Eßzimmer* etc. and start with *dem* which occurs more often in this context than *der*. A simple colour code (e.g. *Küche* marked with a red dot) may also help pupils to get it right.
- *Gegenüber* will be more easily explained using the house plan.

- Do plenty of work with where pupils sit in class to present these positions.
- Worksheets Set 2, 1 and 2 can then link a room and its position.
- A lot of activities where pupils match pictures to information will be needed here.

Assignment

This could be recorded or written as appropriate.

4(v) Furniture

- Do the flashcard presentation and Worksheets Set 1 using only five or six items at a time.
- Most of the games can be used, but in particular bingo (all levels) and beetle.
- Rooms can be built up in the same way as the house was in (iii).
- If teachers wish they can add furniture/appliances for the bathroom and kitchen but it was felt that, for most pupils, the topic already had sufficient content.

Assignment

This could be used as a cross-curricular activity with technology.

An extra dimension can be added to this by providing pupils with a German mail order catalogue (*Quelle* or *Neckermann*) or with brochures from furniture stores; pupils are given a sum of money or spending limit with which they furnish a room with furniture from the catalogue. Furthermore, the type of room can be specified, e.g. a teenager's bedroom, a student's bedsit, a holiday apartment in Spain, etc.

4(vi) Inside the home

- This topic allows all of the information from the rest of the module to be drawn together in a fairly detailed project.
- Write the colour names on coloured card for flashcards.
- All previous activities can be re-used, encouraging pupils to give as much information as possible about their house including rooms and furniture.
- Worksheets Set 2, 1–3 can be used for writing or reading (give either pictures or words) using rooms and items of furniture, and for gap-filling if sheet 3 is included.
- The higher levels of bingo here are also appropriate.
- Pupils should be encouraged to talk about their last assignment, an ideal room.
- Discussion can then follow on their own homes and rooms and, in particular, their own bedroom.

Assignment

This has been left open in order to encourage pupils to choose their own topic to round off the module; this can be presented in either written or spoken form.

MODULE 5 A visit to Germany

Timescale
1 term

Areas of experience
A   B   C   E

Topics / Communicative objectives

Topics	Communicative objectives
(i) Getting there	Understanding and naming means of getting to Germany
(ii) Shops	Understanding and naming types of shop in Germany
(iii) Money	Operating with German money
(iv) Snacks	Understanding and asking for food items
(v) Buying food	Asking for food for a picnic or snack

Assignments
Map with travel routes marked

Design and make labels for shops

Display of labelled foods

Make shopping list for a picnic

Set up classroom shop/café

Shopkeeper/customer scene

Programme of study (part 1): Examples
1   Communicating in the target language
   (a) communicate with each other in pairs and groups and with the teacher
   (b) use language for real purposes
   (c) develop understanding and skills through a range of language activities
2   Language skills
   (a) listen attentively for gist and detail
3   Language learning skills and knowledge of language
   (a) learn by heart phrases and short extracts
4   Cultural awareness
   (e) recognise cultural attitudes as expressed in language e.g. forms of address

Cross-curricular opportunities

Designing and making	Design and Technology
Shopping and money	Maths
Planning and sharing	PSE

Opportunities for assessment

Respond to flashcards	AT1:1; AT2:1,2
Understand names of shops/put in order heard	AT1:1
Play games using shop/food names	AT1:1,2; AT2:1,2
Take part in shop dialogue	AT1:1,2; AT2:1,2,3
Complete shop wordsearch	AT3:1
Put written dialogue in correct order	AT3:2,3
Label transport/shop pictures	AT4:1
Write/complete shop dialogue	AT4:1,2,3
Write shopping list	AT4:1,2

Module 5 A visit to Germany

Topic (i) Getting there

Topic
(i) Getting there

Communicative objective
Understanding and naming means of getting to Germany

Linguistic objectives (examples)
Wie kommt man nach Deutschland?

Man kann fliegen.

> *mit der Fähre fahren.*

> *mit dem Auto fahren.*

> *mit dem Bus fahren.*

> *mit dem Zug fahren.*

Ich fliege.

Ich fahre mit dem Auto/mit der Fähre etc.

> *nach England.*

>> *Schottland.*

>> *Holland.*

>> *Belgien.*

>> *Frankreich.*

>> *London.*

>> *Berlin.*

>> *Österreich.*

> *in die Schweiz.*

von. . . bis nach. . . und dann nach. . .

eine Stunde (Std.).

zwei Stunden.

60 Minuten.

90 Min.

Activities
- Flashcard presentation
- Mimes and sound effects for means of travel
- Recognizing means of travel from brochures and categorizing
- Drawing/labelling transport
- Worksheets Set 1, 1–4
- Wordsearch
- OHT putting on ferry routes/air route
- Marking a route on a map (with symbols of transport) from information given (spoken or written)
- Ordering jumbled-up sentences describing a journey (with the help of a map)

Resources
- Worksheets Set 1, 1–4
- Transport flashcards
- Map of routes, template 11
- Snap/Pelmanism, template 1
- Made-up wordsearch, template 4b
- Transport cue cards
- OHT map with routes as overlays, template 11

- Brochures from cross-channel ferries for pictures of ferries/hovercraft, etc. or magazine pictures
- Song cassette

Assignments
Enlarged map with ferry and air routes marked showing duration of journey and illustrated with pictures of means of travel and other items linked with travel, e.g. cases, bags, etc.

Module 5 A visit to Germany

Topic (ii) Shops

Topic
(ii) Shops

Communicative objective
Understanding and naming types of shop in Germany

Linguistic objectives (examples)
der Laden (ö)/das Geschäft (-e)

der Markt

der Supermarkt

das Einkaufszentrum

die Bäckerei

die Konditorei

die Metzgerei

die Apotheke

der Zeitungsladen

der Schnellimbiß/die Imbißstube

Activities
- Flashcard guessing games
- Matching activities/games
- Worksheets Set 1, 1–4
- Missing letter shop signs
- Jumbled syllable shop signs
- Wordsearch
- Categorizing food, etc. (**not** named at this stage) into correct shop

Resources
- Worksheets Set 1, 1–4
- Shop flashcards
- Food flashcards
- Shop name cards
- Snap/Pelmanism, template 1
- Made-up wordsearch, template 4b
- Blank wordsearch, template 4b
- Shop pictures with letters missing from labels
- Cut-up shop name cards, template 12a-c

- Magazine pictures of food or packets/labels, etc.
- Song cassette

Assignments
Classroom display with shop names above large window (card) for pupils to stick on cut-outs/drawings, categorizing types of food sold in each shop

Module 5 A visit to Germany

Topic (iii) Money

Topic
(iii) Money

Communicative objective
Operating with German money

Linguistic objectives (examples)
deutsches Geld

eine Mark

ein Pfennig

ein Fünfmarkstück (-e)

ein Zehnmarkschein (-e)

ein Zwanzigmarkschein (-e)

Was kostet das?

Hier bitte schön, (7,00 Mark)

Danke, und (50 Pfennig) zurück

(englische) Pfund

billig, billiger

Note:

1,50 DM	*(eine Mark fünfzig)*
2,80 DM	*(zwei Mark achtzig* or *zwei achtzig)*
0,99 DM	*(neunundneunzig Pfennig)*

Activities
• Familiarization with German money

• Sorting coins and/or notes

• Counting money

• Putting together specific amounts of money (e.g. 3,55 DM)

• Giving money and counting out change

• Identifying price labels, Worksheet Set 3, 3

• Simple role plays

Resources
• Worksheets Set 3, 3, filled in with prices

• Pelmanism, template 1, showing coins/notes and prices

• Number cards

• Made-up price tags

• Real, plastic or photocopied currency

• Song cassette

• 'Spielgeld' can be obtained from some banks, in particular from the 'Sparkasse'

Assignments
Working towards the classroom shop or café, and shopkeeper or waiter and customer scene

Module 5 A visit to Germany

Topic (iv) Snacks

Topic
(iv) Snacks

Communicative objective
Understanding and asking for food items

Linguistic objectives (examples)

das Brot

das Brötchen (-)

der Käse

der Schinken

das Käsebrot/das Schinkenbrötchen

die Kekse (mpl)

die Bonbons (mpl)

die Kartoffelchips (mpl)

die Schokolade

das Eis

die Banane (-n)

der Apfel (¨)

die Apfelsine (-n)/die Orange (-n)

die (Wein)trauben (fpl)

die Tomate (-n)

die Wurst

die Bratwurst

die Bockwurst

die Pommes frites

der Tee

der Kaffee

das Bier

die Limo(nade)

das Cola

der Wein

Was kostet das?

Was kostet der/die/das. . . ?

Was kosten die. . . ?

Activities
- Flashcard guessing games
- Matching activities words/pictures
- Worksheets Set 1, 1–4, Set 3, 1–2 to reinforce vocabulary
- Worksheets Set 2, 1–3, linking food with appropriate shops/prices/opinions
- Kim's game
- Pelmanism
- Food bingo
- Sequencing of food asked for, Worksheet Set 3, 3
- Categorizing items into shops (window display)
- Labelling food
- Putting pictures in alphabetical order

Resources
- Worksheets Set 1, 1–4, Set 2, 1–3, Set 3, 1–3
- Food flashcards
- Snap/Pelmanism, template 1
- Dominoes, template 2
- Made-up wordsearch, template 4a or 4b
- Bingo template B7
- Cue cards

- Made-up shopping lists of words with letters missing or pictures
- Tray and objects
- Where possible:
  – empty containers of German food
  – German magazine pictures of food
  – plastic food
  – leaflets from German supermarkets
- Song cassette

Assignments
Display of labelled food, completing the previous assignment of making up shop windows

Shopping list for a picnic

Module 5 A visit to Germany

Topic (v) Buying food

Topic

(v) Buying food

Communicative objective

Asking for food for a picnic or snack

Linguistic objectives (examples)

greetings

Was darf's sein?/Sie wünschen bitte?/Bitte schön?

Ich hätte gern. . ./Ich möchte bitte. . .

eine Packung. . ./zwei Packungen. . .

eine Flasche. . ./zwei Flaschen. . .

eine Dose. . ./zwei Dosen. . .

ein Kilo/zwei Pfund

zwei Kilo. . .

ein Pfund (= 500g)

Wär's das?

Danke, das wär's.

Was macht das, bitte?

Hier, bitte schön.

foods and drinks – see 5(iv)

Activities

- Revise greetings
- Demonstrate asking for required amounts of food
- Matching containers and foods, i.e. appropriateness
- Worksheets Set 2, 1–3, linking amounts/containers with food and drink
- Worksheets Set 2, 5a and 5b, dialogue – build up dialogue
- Bingo – snacks
- Pairwork and groupwork
- Building up dialogues for café or shop

Resources

- Food and drink flashcards
- Bingo, template B8
- Worksheets Set 2, 1–3, 5a and 5b

- As many props as possible for shop/café scene:
  – empty German food packets
  – empty English packets relabelled (by pupils?)
  – plastic food
- Magazine pictures
- Price tags
- Bags for shopping
- Shopping lists
- Plastic cups for café
- Song cassette

Assignments

Set up classroom shop/café

Make up scene with customer and shopkeeper or waiter

Possibly set up a real snack bar one breaktime with filled rolls or sausages (frankfurters) (if available), sweets, crisps, fruit and drinks

---

DEUTSCH? KEIN PROBLEM!

Module 5: A visit to Germany

5(i) Getting there

- You need to do work with maps of all kinds to ensure understanding of the relative positions of England and Germany (and Austria and Switzerland), and to do lots of matching/repetition to get across the German names of the countries.
- We suggest that you add an overlay to template 11 showing the routes most relevant to you and your local area.
- If the map is copied onto an OHT the routes can be overlaid using different colours and, eventually, OHT cut-outs of the means of transport appropriately placed.
- For presentation of the transport vocabulary use all the guessing and matching activities and games.
- Get the pupils to think up mimes and sound-effects for each one to give variety to recognition activities.
- Working with travel brochures, especially cross-Channel ferry information with pictures and details of routes to the Continent will be good general experience for the pupils.

Note: the use of *man kann* here facilitates in a simple way talking about travel to the Continent in general; however, *ich* could be used if teachers prefer. *Man* is useful for any general statements later, e.g. what you can buy in various shops, etc.

Assignment
Using drawings and cut-outs pupils can make a large display about travel to and from Germany, Austria or Switzerland. Pieces of coloured string can indicate the various routes.

5(ii) Shops

- At this point in the visit, the shops are merely being named, not used; although some activities suggest recognition through categorizing items for sale, these need not be named in German yet. For listening or reading practice cognates can be used (e.g. *Tomaten*, *Äpfel*, *Schokolade*, *Eis*, *Kaffee*, etc.) supported by pictures.
- With the large shop name cards (enlarged) you can begin to build up a display of a row of shops on the classroom wall, with a large card beneath each one as the shop window, where pictures can be affixed and labelled.
- Copy the shop signs and blank out some letters to give practice in spelling them; 'which letter is missing?' also gives alphabet practice.
- With the wordsearch, do not overlook the possibility of pupils designing their own for use in class.

Assignment
Building up the large shop wall display (see above).

5(iii) Money

Note: The amount of detail covered in this topic will vary and is at the discretion of the teacher.

- The central point is that pupils should have a basic understanding of German currency.
- They also need to know how much money they would need to cover the cost of an item requested, e.g. if the item is 3,50 DM they would give 4 DM and receive change, i.e. teach them to 'round up'.
- It is sometimes helpful to pupils' understanding of the approximate value of coins, etc. to compare them with the English, i.e. shape, size, colour, etc. An envelope containing a mixture of German coins and notes can be given to pairs of pupils with the first task being to sort the money (i.e. all the one-Mark coins together, the two-Mark coins and so on). After sorting they can then arrange the coins and notes according to their value starting with the smallest denomination and finishing with the largest. Finally the money can be counted to establish the value of the contents of each envelope. The next step could then be to ask pupils to use their money to put together exact sums (e.g. 3,50 DM) using the coins/notes provided.
- Now they can act out very basic dialogues: *Was kostet das? – 4 Mark. Bitte schön, 5 Mark. – Danke, und eine Mark zurück.*
- Make up price tags to get pupils used to saying German amounts.
- Some pupils will be able to do work based on the exchange rate, i.e. using a calculator to help them work out how much individual German coins/notes are worth in English money; or they can find out the prices of some everyday foods or household goods from the local supermarket and compare them with items found in advertisements from German supermarkets. Comparisons could be introduced here (orally/written) e.g. *Brot ist billiger in England. Schokolade ist billiger in Deutschland.* The same vocabulary can be used as in 5(ii). Alternatively, this activity could be done in 5(iv) once some foods have been taught.
- Ideally, all pupils should have a basic understanding of what the exchange rate is and how prices can be worked out in English money.
- Because of the importance, when going to a German-speaking country, of understanding prices over the counter, (i.e. spoken), plenty of listening activities need to be done with prices, initially by

Teaching notes 5

ticking the correct one of three or four and eventually writing the prices they hear in figures.

Assignment

Simple dialogues and making/labelling or pricing goods realistically in preparation for the next assignment.

5(iv) Snacks

Note: teachers are advised to use the food items which they feel are most appropriate to the group of pupils. These have been presented in three groups: (a) groceries/snacks, (b) drinks, (c) fruit and vegetables.

- This is a good opportunity for pupils to handle things – empty packets or plastic bottles, etc. You can always re-label British items in German.
- Do not present too many new words at once and do not over-use the basic worksheets – other activities such as picture/word shopping lists would practise the same reading, understanding, writing skills and give variety, which is vital.
- Kim's game is a good one here, particularly if one category of foods is used at a time.
- Putting pictures in alphabetical order is an introduction to dictionary skills – do not give more than five or six at a time and encourage a little rap or tune to be made up when the list is correct.
- Although not suggested as a core activity, pupils could revise likes/dislikes here using either the personal *ich mag. . ./ich mag keine. . .* or *ich mag. . . nicht* sheets, template 9, or the listening worksheet, Set 2, sheet 4.
- The boundary between the shop and café has been left deliberately vague here since pupils are simply practising asking for what they want, no matter what the situation.

Assignment

- The display of labelled foods could be empty English packets re-labelled in German, or labelled pictures (drawn or cut out).

- Using supermarket leaflets showing foods and prices, pupils can make a list of the foods and drinks they want to buy for a picnic for four people (they have 100 DM to spend).

5(v) Buying Food

- Revise greetings for the eventual role play.
- Learning the vocabulary for containers, amounts and numbers for shopping is important because pupils also learn what is appropriate.
- More vocabulary for a picnic or snack can be taken from the full food list if required.
- Using picture cards (snap size) get pupils to match containers/weights and foods.
- The double worksheets, Set 2, can then be used to practise this.
- It would be nice to record pairs or groups on cassette and even on video.

Dialogue pattern (guidance only):
- *Guten Tag.*
- *Guten Tag. Bitte schön?*
- *Eine Dose Cola, bitte.*
- *Wär's das?*
- *Nein, und ein Eis, bitte.*
- *Wär's das?*
- *Ja, danke. Was macht das, bitte?*
- *Drei Mark.*
- *Bitte schön.*
- *Danke. Wiedersehen.*
- *Auf Wiedersehen.*

Note: Break the dialogue down into small sections and practise these thoroughly, gradually building up to the whole conversation. Use symbols and pictures if necessary to help pupils remember the order of things. Some pupils get confused by the different uses of *bitte (schön)*. Practise giving – *Hier bitte* – and receiving – *danke* (and the reply *bitte*) – with flashcards or objects, at every opportunity as part of classroom language.

DEUTSCH? KEIN PROBLEM!

MODULE 6 At home

Timescale
1 term

Areas of experience
A   B   D

Topics and Communicative objectives

Topics	Communicative objectives
(i) Family hobbies	Exchanging information about how family members spend their free time
(ii) Meals	Exchanging information about meals
(iii) Who does what?	Exchanging information about the division of household tasks
(iv) At the table	Coping at mealtimes

Assignments
Survey of home hobbies/graph

Role play at meal table

Family album with cassette

Programme of study (part 1): Examples
1   Communicating in the target language
    (a) communicate with each other in pairs and groups and with the teacher
    (c) develop understanding and skills through a range of language activities
2   Language skills
    (a) listen attentively for gist and detail
    (e) ask for and give information
4   Cultural awareness
    (c) consider their own culture and compare it

Cross-curricular opportunities

Graphs	Maths
Family life	} PSE
Different types of families	}

Opportunities for assessment

Respond to flashcards	AT1:1; AT2:1,2
Understand hobbies/tasks	AT1:1,2
Ask/answer questions about what other people do	AT1:1,2; AT2:1,2
Say a few sentences about what people do	AT2:2,3
Match words to pictures	AT3:2
Build sentences using cut-up sentence cards	AT3:2,3
Copy sentences about tasks/hobbies	AT4:2
Write simple sentences about tasks/hobbies	AT4:3

Module 6 At home

Topic (i) Family hobbies

Topic
(i) Family hobbies

Communicative objective
Exchanging information on how family members spend their time

Linguistic objectives (examples)

Was macht deine Mutti   am Wochenende?

          deine Schwester

          dein Vati

          dein Bruder

Er/Sie macht (gern) Sport.

     sieht (gern) fern.

     hört (gern) Musik.

     arbeitet (gern) im Garten.

     spielt (gern) mit dem Computer.

     bastelt (gern) am Auto.

     geht (gern) aus/ins Pub/tanzen, etc.

     liest (gern) (Zeitung/Zeitschriften/Krimis/ Comics, etc.*)*

Activities
- Revise members of family from 2(i)
- Presentation of hobbies
- Mime and say
- Match words and pictures
- Talking about what other people do
- Worksheets Set 1 and Set 2, linking family members with hobbies
- Wordsearch
- Pairwork – gap-filling, using Worksheet Set 2, 3
- Copy-writing
- Sentence-building
- Writing simple sentences

Resources
- Worksheets Set 1, 1–4, Set 2, 1–3
- Flashcards – the house
          – family
          – hobbies
          – some target language verbs from topic 1(iv)
- Speech bubbles, template 7
- Made-up wordsearch, template 4b
- Pelmanism, template 1
- Cue cards
- Dominoes, template 2

- Magazine pictures or advertisements of activities
- Cut-up sentence cards
- Family name cards
- Song cassette

Assignments
Picture and caption display to show pupils' family interests

Survey of family hobbies

Module 6 At home

Topic (ii) Meals

Topic
(ii) Meals

Communicative objective
Exchanging information about meals

Linguistic objectives (examples)

das Frühstück

das Mittagessen

das Abendbrot/das Abendessen

nach der Schule

zwischendurch

Wann ist das Frühstück/Mittagessen/Abendessen?

Das (Frühstück) ist um 8 Uhr.

Wo ißt du dein Frühstück?

Ich esse (mein Frühstück) in der Küche.
                        im Eßzimmer.
                        im Wohnzimmer.
                        in der Schule.

Ich esse beim Fernsehen.

Was ißt/trinkst du zum Frühstück?

Ich esse. . . und ich trinke. . .

die Cornflakes (mit Milch/mit Zucker)
der Toast (mit Butter/mit Marmelade)
ein Ei (zwei Eier)   *der Fisch*
der Orangensaft   *das Gemüse*
nichts   *die Erbsen (fpl)*
                              die Karotten (fpl)
die Suppe   *die Bohnen (fpl)*
die Kartoffeln (fpl)   *die Pizza*
der Reis   *der Salat*
die Nudeln (fpl)   *der Hamburger*
das Fleisch   *das Wasser*
das Hähnchen
                              das Brot

See also Module 5, Topic (iv) Snacks.

- make a choice from the foods given under snack foods in Module 5, Topic (iv), including something appropriate for each meal. The amount of vocabulary included here is at the teacher's discretion.

Activities
- Presentation of meals with appropriate times
- Linking meals with food – reading, speaking, writing
- Linking meals with appropriate rooms
- Worksheets Set 1
- Worksheets Set 2
- Wordsearch
- Sentence-building orally and written from pictures/words
- Kim's game
- Beetle

Resources
- Worksheets Set 1, 1–4
- Worksheets Set 2, 1–3
- Flashcards – food
       – meals
       – three mealtimes
       – rooms
- Beetle – sets of food to make meals
- Made-up wordsearch, template 4b
- Snap picture/word cards, template 1
- Cue cards

- Magazine pictures for collage
- Appropriate empty packets, etc.
- Song cassette

Assignments
Labelled collage or drawings of typical meals for display

Module 6 At home

Topic (iii) Who does what?

Topic

(iii) Who does what?

Communicative objective

Exchanging information about the division of household tasks

Linguistic objectives (examples)

Wer macht sauber?

macht die Betten?

macht die Wäsche?

macht das Geschirr?

macht das Essen?

macht den Garten?

macht die Einkäufe?

alles

nichts

Ich

mein Vati

meine Mutti

mein Bruder

meine Schwester

Was machst du?

Ich mache. . .

Was macht dein Bruder/deine Schwester, etc.?

Er/Sie macht. . .

Activities

- Worksheets Set 1
- Miming activities
- Matching games
- Pairwork – information gap, Worksheet Set 2, 3
- Making picture and caption display
- Listening to **who** does **what**. Worksheet Set 3, 3
- Singing: make up a rap or use a well-known tune for household tasks

Resources

- Worksheets Set 1, 1–4, Set 2, 1–3
- Worksheet Set 3, 3, made-up with household tasks
- Household task flashcards
- Made-up wordsearch, template 4b
- Pelmanism – household tasks words and pictures, template 1
- Cards for sentence-building
- Noughts and crosses, templates 3a and 3b, and small OHT pictures
- Cue cards

- Any appropriate props
- Song cassette

Assignments

Pictures and cassette describing own family's division of household tasks, with sound effects made by pupils' use of props and voices, etc.

Module 6 At home

Topic (iv) At the table

Topic
(iv) At the table

Communicative objective
Coping at mealtimes

Linguistic objectives (examples)

Bitte (den) Tisch decken!

Auf dem Tisch ist/sind. . .

ein Teller/zwei Teller

ein Messer/zwei Messer

ein Löffel/zwei Löffel

eine Gabel/zwei Gabeln

eine Serviette/zwei Servietten

ein Glas/zwei Gläser

Guten Appetit!

Kann ich bitte [die Butter] haben?

Die Butter, bitte?

Hier, bitte.

Danke.

Möchtest du. . . ?

Ja, bitte.

Nein, danke.

Noch etwas?

Noch Salat?

Danke, ich bin satt.

Schmeckt's?

Ja, (das schmeckt) prima.

Ja, (das ist) lecker.

Activities
- Laying the table:
  – present vocabulary with objects if possible
  – pupils take turns in placing correct objects, then number of objects, on table
- Make wall display
- Speaking/writing *Auf dem Tisch sind. . .* revising numbers and new vocabulary
- Group lay table, one member does commentary
- Revision of food – likes/dislikes, Worksheet Set 2, 4, *ich esse gern/ich trinke gern. . ./ich esse nicht gern. . .* Leave out preference (*lieber*) if necessary
- Practise questions and answers
- Noughts and crosses
- Beetle
- Kim's game
- Bingo – laid table

Resources
- Food flashcards
- Table setting flashcards
- Noughts and crosses, templates 3a and 3b
- Beetle, template 1 (sets of place settings)
- Kim's game – table laid
- Bingo template B10

- Paper/plastic tableware
- Empty food packets, etc.
- Cut-out magazine pictures of food
- Real German food

Assignments
Classroom display of table laid ready for meal

A real or simulated mealtime situation; this could be recorded on video or audio cassette

Module 6: At home

6(i) Family hobbies

- Use the flashcards from 2(i) to revise the members of the family.
- Revise the use of *er/sie*; this could be just a short activity in class: *Wie heißt er?* – teacher points and another pupil replies, *Er heißt. . .* Then *Wie alt ist Darren?* – *Er ist. . .* etc.
- Introduce the new language with flashcards or on the OHP, building up to *Was macht er/sie? Er/sie hört Musik.*
- Pupils can complete worksheets Set 1 initially using the third person only.
- Use template 2 to play dominoes working with split sentences, e.g. *im Garten/Vati hört/Musik/Meine Schwester arbeitet*, etc.
- Use the double boxes of the Set 2 worksheets to build sentences.
- Snap-sized cards with names, verbs and nouns could be given out for pupils to make up sentences about a make-believe family. To demonstrate understanding they can then draw or match pictures of these.
- Questions can now be used to encourage pupils to talk about their own family.
- With some pupils it might also be possible to introduce *gern/nicht gern*. Once the verbs and sentences have been practised, add *gern/nicht gern* using the familiar heart symbols. Begin with visuals to elicit *Er macht Sport* etc. Then adding one of the heart symbols: *Macht er Sport gern oder nicht gern?* inviting a short response: *gern* or *nicht gern*.
- The next step could be for pupils to sort sentences (heard or read) in two columns under the appropriate heart symbols. From there, pupils can practise the full response to the question *Was macht dein Vati gern (am Wochenende)? Er macht gern Sport*.

Note: Using the first person as well as the third person must remain at the teacher's discretion. It is possible to start with the first person and then to proceed to use the third person, but pupils will need plenty of practice to help them distinguish between the two verb forms (listening discrimination/matching and gap-filling activities, and possibly a verb chart pupils can refer to when necessary).

Assignment

- Using pictures of adverts from magazines (teenage ones are particularly useful) the pupils fill in blank speech bubbles to match pictures and make a display.
- A survey of family pastimes – the simplest format would be to set pastimes against family members, so pupils put ticks in boxes as they get information from each other; a graph could then be made of the most popular pastimes with particular family members.

6(ii) Meals

Note: it is **not** intended to introduce time fully here; however, three typical times of meals each day could be taught as items of vocabulary and simply used to clarify which meal is meant.

- Presentation of meals with simple times if desired.
- With the emphasis in this topic on **meals**, keep the food chosen to introduce/revise vocabulary appropriate to typical meals of your pupils, otherwise the vocabulary will become too large.
- Make good use of the Set 1 worksheets, wordsearch and bingo for the introduction and practice of this food vocabulary.
- The double worksheets (Set 2) are useful to link meal/place eaten, meal/food eaten.
- Again, with Kim's game, try to group foods typical to a particular meal to help pupils recognize meals and begin to categorize food in a different way from in Module 5.
- Pelmanism – if you use meal cards and food cards the game can be that the cards are only kept (won) if the food is appropriate to that meal. Encourage speaking during the game. Pupil 1: *Frühstück* (as they turn it up). Pupil 2: *Pommes frites – nein, das ist Mittagessen*.
- Beetle too can have various groups of six cards to make up the possibilities for all four meals, so that pupils can then categorize the food under meals.

Assignment

All of this important categorization of food can then be used to make a display of typical meals, with collage or drawings, with labels.

6(iii) Who does what?

- Beside the usual flashcard presentation and guessing games, mimes and props will give added interest and amusement here.
- Worksheets Set 1, then matching games, will reinforce the new vocabulary.
- A change from the usual listening activity could be to use sounds of activities for recognition – pupils can be encouraged to make the sound effects, with props, behind a screen/cupboard door.
- The double worksheets, Set 2, can link family members to tasks and lead to speaking, reading or writing.
- An information-gap pairwork exercise can be made using the above sheets by giving one pupil half A of the picture and the other half B of the sentence.

Assignment
This is meant to be fun – but also a lot of useful social education is learnt here!

6(iv) At the table
- Present the vocabulary with objects if possible as this is a good opportunity for movement and for manipulating objects.
- Give plenty of opportunity for individuals or groups to lay a table. This revises recognizing numbers in a real situation too.
- Kim's game will help memorization.
- Noughts and crosses could be played flat on a table with pupils having to either say the correct item that is placed in a square or replace it with the correct cue card, or vice-versa.
- Beetle too can get a new perspective here with pupils actually building up their place-setting.
- At this stage the food items are mostly revised, although the class may be ready for some extra vocabulary to be presented. Use plastic food, empty packets, magazine pictures (on card and laminated if possible) and, of course, real German food if it is available and can be funded.
- *Kann ich bitte. . . haben? Möchtest du. . . ? Noch etwas?* should all be practised by pairs and groups with either pictures or realia to handle.

Assignment
- The table laid for a meal can be a three-dimensional wall display using paper plates, plastic cutlery, etc. which can be glued or sellotaped on.
- The meal might be more feasible if done on a cross-curricular basis or in conjunction with the school canteen. A German breakfast is relatively easy to organize, is quite different from most English pupils' breakfast and offers scope for a great variety of language.

MODULE 7 Looking after a visitor

Timescale

1 term

Areas of experience

A   B   C   E

Topics / Communicative objectives

Topics	Communicative objectives
(i) My family	Introducing a German-speaking visitor to members of the family
(ii) My home	Showing a visitor around the home
(iii) Local facilities	Explaining what there is to do in the area
(iv) Local transport	Discussing the best way of getting around

Assignments

Plan of home with labels

Plan of town with facilities labelled

Design and make a poster to advertise a facility

Plan map showing routes/transport facilities

Programme of study (part 1): Examples

1   Communicating in the target language
 (a)   communicate with each other in pairs and groups and with the teacher
 (c)   develop understanding and skills through a range of language activities
2   Language skills
 (a)   listen attentively for gist and detail
 (e)   ask for and give information
 (k)   copy words, phrases and sentences
3   Language learning skills and knowledge of language
 (a)   learn by heart phrases and short extracts

Cross-curricular opportunities

Designing and making	Design and Technology
Geography	
Understanding the needs of others	PSE

Opportunities for assessment

Respond to flashcards	AT1:1; AT2:1,2
Understand names of facilities	AT1:1
Ask/answer questions about facilities	AT1:1,2; AT2:1,2,3
Say what there is to do in a town	AT2:2,3
Match words to pictures of facilities	AT3:1
Label town plan	AT4:1
Write simple sentences about what there is to do in a town	AT4:2,3

Module 7 Looking after a visitor

Topic (i) My family

Topic
(i) My family

Communicative objective
Introducing a German visitor to members of the family

Linguistic objectives (examples)

Guten Tag!

Hallo!

Freut mich.

Wie geht's?

Wie war die Reise?

Danke, gut.

Das (hier) ist meine Mutter.

       meine Schwester.

       meine Oma.

       mein Vater.

       mein Bruder.

       mein Opa.

       + see teaching notes

(Und) das ist meine Katze.

       mein Hund.

Er/Sie heißt. . .

Activities
- Revision of family from Module 2
- Wordsearch
- Beetle (make up family)
- Role plays using other names

Resources
- Ready-made wordsearch, template 4b
- Beetle (family), template 1
- Resources as for Module 2 for revision of family

- Props for dressing up
- Name cards for role plays (English first and surnames for English family as well as German name for visitor)
- Song cassette

Assignments
Presentation of a short play showing a family meeting a German visitor

Module 7 Looking after a visitor | Topic (ii) My home

Topic
(ii) My home

Communicative objective
Showing a visitor around the home

Linguistic objectives (examples)

Hier ⎱ *ist die Küche.*
Das ⎰ *die Toilette.*

das Bad.

das Wohnzimmer.

das Eßzimmer.

das Gästezimmer.

dein Zimmer.

*das Schlafzimmer von meinen Eltern/
Muttis und Vatis Zimmer.*

das Zimmer von meinem Bruder.

Peters Zimmer.

das Zimmer von meiner Schwester.

Tanjas Zimmer.

Oh ja!

Sehr schön.

Oh hübsch!

Ja, danke.

Aha!

Und (was ist) das?

Activities
- Flashcard/OHP games for revision – hiding/guessing/naming
- Matching games – snap, Pelmanism
- Beetle, rooms in the house
- Game – which room is missing? (OHT or cards)
- Pairwork guessing game with picture cards face down
- Worksheets Set 2, 1–2 for bedrooms belonging to members of the family

Resources
- Worksheets Set 2, 1–2
- Flashcards – family
  rooms
- Bingo, template B6
- Beetle, template 1 (sets of rooms)
- Made-up wordsearch, template 4b
- OHT house and furniture
- Cue cards

- Cut-out pictures and labels
- Magazine pictures of rooms
- Song cassette

Assignments
Plan or set of pictures of own home with room labels

Scene with visitor being shown around the home

DEUTSCH? KEIN PROBLEM!

Module 7 Looking after a visitor

Topic (iii) Local facilities

Topic
(iii) Local facilities

Communicative objective
Explaining what there is to do in the area

Linguistic objectives (examples)

In [Southampton] gibt es. . .

Was gibt es (hier) in Southampton?

Southampton hat. . .

Es gibt (hier) ein Kino/zwei Kinos.

> *ein Schwimmbad.*
>
> *ein Eisstadion.*
>
> *ein (Fußball)stadion.*
>
> *ein Sportzentrum.*
>
> *ein Museum/zwei Museen.*
>
> *eine Disko(thek)/viele Diskos/Diskotheken.*
>
> *einen Park/viele Parks.*
>
> *einen Hafen.*
>
> *einen Strand.*
>
> *viele Cafés.*
>
> *viele Restaurants.*
>
> *viele Geschäfte.*
>
> *eine Altstadt.*

Activities

- Flashcard/OHP games
- Matching activities/games
- Worksheets Set 1, 1–4, Set 3, 1–2
- Worksheets Set 2 linking town and facility
- Miming
- Labelling town plan
- Look for information in German brochures
- Interpret information for German-speaking visitor in English
- Write simple sentences about what there is in a town
- Bingo with town outline and facilities
- IT opportunity

Resources

- Worksheets Set 1, 1–4, Set 2, 1–2, Set 3, 1–2
- Town flashcards
- Bingo, template B9
- Pelmanism/snap, template 1
- Dominoes, template 2
- Town plan and pictures to glue on, template B9
- Cue cards

- Brochures from German towns (or English brochures to explain to German-speaking visitors)
- Song cassette

Assignments

Plan of town with facilities labelled

Brochure to advertise a town

Poster to advertise a facility in the town

Make a tape about the facilities in your town to help blind tourists

Module 7 Looking after a visitor

Topic (iv) Local transport

Topic
(iv) Local transport

Communicative objective
Discussing the best way of getting around

Linguistic objectives (examples)
Möchtest du nach Winchester?

ins Kino?

ins Schwimmbad?

ins Museum?

ins Eisstadion?

in die Disko?

in die (Alt)stadt?

zum Strand?

Sollen wir. . . fahren/gehen?

Oh ja, prima!

Ja, gute Idee!

(Nein) ich möchte lieber. . .

Wie kommen wir dahin?

(Wir fahren) mit dem Bus.

mit dem Zug.

mit dem Fahrrad.

mit dem Auto.

(Wir gehen) zu Fuß.

Gut.

Okay.

Activities
- Flashcards, etc. to revise known transport words and present new ones
- Pairwork – questions and answers suggesting what to do
- Pairwork – questions and answers using place and transport cards face down
- Role play
- Guess the rule

Resources
- Worksheets Set 2, 1–3 linking places and transport
- Transport flashcards also from 5(i)
- Pictures and words for sentence-building
- Cue cards

- Large town plan
- Toy vehicles to use with the above if possible
- Song cassette

Assignments
Role play deciding what to do and how to get there, linking 7(iii) and 7(iv)

Module 7: Looking after a visitor

7(i) My family
- Revise family members using resources from Module 2.
- If required, for children from split families, it may be useful to have the following available: *mein Stiefvater/meine Stiefmutter/mein Stiefbruder*, etc. for step-parents, step-brother, etc. and *mein Halbbruder, meine Halbschwester* for half-brother half-sister.
- Games like beetle and a wordsearch will also help to revise vocabulary.

Assignment
- Groupwork for role play: a German visitor being introduced into a British home – have props and name cards to complete the simulation.
- If a video is available to film the play, this would be a wonderful motivation.

Note: if pupils cannot manage *Er/sie heißt* they can say *meine Mutter heißt*, etc.

7(ii) My home
- Again, this is largely revision of 4(iii), so use a variety of activities to revise rooms in the house.
- Family flashcards and name cards are needed to present *das Zimmer von meinem Bruder*; this construction can be avoided by using names, e.g. *Liams Zimmer, Vatis Zimmer, Muttis und Vatis Zimmer* etc. This can be practised with the double-box worksheets Set 2, 1–2.
- It is possible to teach pupils some simple responses to what they are shown so that dialogues can develop.

Assignment
- The assignments are such that the scene suggested can build on the one in 7(i), and the set of labelled pictures may be done by pupils who find the concept of a plan too difficult.

7(iii) Local facilities
- As a new and significant set of vocabulary, these words must be thoroughly, but only gradually, presented and practised.

- Worksheets Set 1, wordsearch, bingo and matching games will reinforce vocabulary.
- Double-box worksheets (Set 2) will encourage sentences: *In* [town] *gibt es. . .*
- A large town plan can gradually be built up as a display with places being added as they are learnt.
- The thrill of just looking at brochures from Germany, Austria or Switzerland is a good enough reason for sending off to various towns in these countries, but they will also extend reading skills with truly (and obviously) authentic materials.
- Even British brochures with town plans and descriptions will be interesting and will allow some simple interpreting to take place.

Assignments
- This topic really lends itself to projects of various kinds. Posters and brochures can be individual or pair work; the town plan could involve a whole group; and the cassette could be spoken by one pupil and scripted by others.

7(iv) Local transport
- Revise known transport words from 5(i) and present new ones.
- If you can make a table town plan and use toy cars, buses, etc. this whole section comes to life!
- Encourage the simple dialogue by giving out place and transport Pelmanism cards and as each pair are turned up pupil 1 says *Sollen wir ins Kino gehen?* and pupil 2 replies *Ja gut, wir fahren mit dem Bus*.
- Develop this by pupil 2 also having to pick up a place and say *Nein, ich möchte lieber ins Schwimmbad*, etc.

Assignment
The role play will have been developed through the preceding activities.

MODULE 8 Enjoying life

Timescale
1 term

Areas of experience
A   B

Topics / Communicative objectives

Topics	Communicative objectives
(i) Favourite pastimes	Exchanging information about sports and hobbies
(ii) Going out with friends	Making arrangements to meet and go out
(iii) Parts of the body	Understanding and naming parts of the body
(iv) Health	Asking and answering questions about personal health

Assignments
Design and make a poster advertising a sport/hobby

Survey/database of class interests

Exercise routine with instructions in German, maybe with a video

Collage – body and labels using cut-up magazines

Programme of study (part 1): Examples
1   Communicating in the target language
  (a) communicate with each other in pairs and groups and with the teacher
  (c) develop understanding and skills through a range of language activities
  (f) discuss own interests and compare them with those of others
2   Language skills
  (d) ask and answer questions and give instructions
3   Language learning skills and knowledge of language
  (a) learn by heart phrases and short extracts

Cross-curricular opportunities

Designing and making	Design and Technology
Me (my body and how it works)	PSE
Database work	} Maths
Measuring and graph work	

Opportunities for assessment

Respond to flashcards	AT1:1; AT2:1
Understand names of hobbies/sports	AT1:1
Understand other people's opinions on hobbies/sports	AT1:1,2,3
Ask/answer questions on hobbies/sports	AT1:1,2; AT2:1,2
Ask/answer survey questions	AT1:2; AT2:1,2,3
Say what your hobbies are	AT2:2,3
Put written dialogue in correct order	AT3:2,3
Write/complete dialogue	AT4:1,2,3
Dialogue/conversation	AT2:2,3
Match words and pictures of hobbies/sports/body parts	AT3:1,2
Follow written instructions to cut out and make body	AT3:2,3,4
Label pictures	AT4:1,2
Complete/write speech bubbles	AT4:1,2,3

DEUTSCH? KEIN PROBLEM!

Module 8 Enjoying life

Topic (i) Favourite pastimes

Topic
(i) Favourite pastimes

Communicative objective
Exchanging information about sports and hobbies

Linguistic objectives (examples)

Was machst du gern am Wochenende?

abends?

nach der Schule?

Ich spiele (gern) Badminton.

Basketball.

Fußball.

Kricket.

Rugby.

Snooker.

Tennis.

mit dem Computer.

Ich gehe (gern) angeln.

reiten.

radfahren.

tanzen.

einkaufen.

ins Kino.

zum Fußball.

aus.

Spielst du gern. . . ?

Gehst du gern. . . ?

Ja, sehr gern.

Ja, ganz gern.

Nein, nicht so gern.

Ich lese (gern).

Ich höre (gern) Musik.

Ich sehe (gern) fern.

Ich male (gern).

Wieviele Personen. . . ?

Activities
- Flashcard activities
- Worksheets Set 1, 1–4
- Miming
- Matching games – snap, Pelmanism, dominoes
- Noughts and crosses
- Dialogues (use only *Spielst du gern. . . ?* or *Gehst du gern. . . ?* with short answers, *Ja, sehr gern/Nein, nicht so gern*)
- Worksheet Set 2, 5b
- Picture profile of likes/dislikes
- Class survey with oral/written follow-up, template 10

Resources
- Worksheets Set 1, 1–4, Set 2, 1–4
- Sports/hobbies flashcards
- Pelmanism/snap, template 1
- Dominoes, template 2
- Noughts and crosses, templates 3a and 3b
- Made-up wordsearch, template 4b
- Blank wordsearch, template 4a
- Likes/dislikes sheet, template 9
- Cue cards
- Template 10 (survey)

- Song cassette

Assignments
Poster advertising sport or hobby

A labelled picture profile of personal interests

Class survey with findings presented in form of a bar graph

Module 8 Enjoying life

Topic (ii) Going out with friends

Topic
(ii) Going out with friends

Communicative objective
Making arrangements to meet and go out

Linguistic objectives (examples)
Hallo?

Hallo, hier ist der/die (+ name)

Ich gehe. . . , kommst du mit?

Wann?/(Um) wieviel Uhr?

Um + time

Wo (treffen wir uns)?

Bei mir.

Bei dir.

Ja, prima.

Ja, okay.

Activities
- Revise clock (full hour and maybe half hour); question and answers template 8, worksheets Set 1, 1–4
- Flashcard activities
- Miming guessing games
- Pairwork – dialogues with cue cards
- Sentence building
- Worksheet Set 3, 3

Resources
- Worksheets Set 1, 1–4
- Activity flashcards
- Cue cards
- Templates 7 and 8
- Worksheet Set 2, 5a

- Clock
- (Toy) telephones (a pencil case with a pen sticking out or similar makes an excellent mobile!)

Assignments
Make up and perform a sketch inviting someone out; this could be on audio or video

Module 8 Enjoying life

Topic (iii) Parts of the body

Topic
(iii) Parts of the body

Communicative objective
Understanding and naming parts of the body

Linguistic objectives (examples)
der Kopf

der Hals

der Zahn (˝e)

das Ohr (-en)

das Auge (-n)

die Nase

der Mund

der Körper

der Arm (-e)

die Hand (˝e)

der Finger (-)

das Bein (-e)

das Knie (-)

der Fuß (˝e)

der Rücken

der Bauch

Activities
- Recognition practice games:
  - point and say
  - *Walter sagt*
- Exercising – see teaching notes page 149
- Worksheets Set 1, 1–4
- Beetle
- Make own wordsearch
- Following instructions to cut out parts of body or choose ready-made cut-outs
- IT opportunity
- Bingo, template B12

Resources
- Worksheets Set 1, 1–4
- Body flashcards
- Pelmanism/snap/beetle, template 1
- Dominoes, template 2
- Noughts and crosses, templates 3a and 3b
- Made-up wordsearch, template 4b
- Blank wordsearch, template 4a
- Bingo, template B12
- Cue cards

- Magazines to cut up
- Song cassette

Assignments
Collage – body and labels using cut-up magazine pictures

Exercise routine in German (possibly using keyboard rhythm or well-known tune)

Module 8 Enjoying life

Topic (iv) Health

Topic
(iv) Health

Communicative objective
Asking and answering questions about personal health

Linguistic objectives (examples)
Wie geht's?

Gut, danke.

Es geht, danke.

Nicht so gut.

mein/meine. . . tut weh.

Aua!

Was ist los?

Ach du Arme/Armer! (You poor thing!) (optional)

Gute Besserung! (optional)

Activities
- Presentation of *. . .tut weh*
- Mimes of pains
- Labelling pictures*
- Completing speech bubbles*
- Sticking plasters (on picture) to show where pain is*

*Combination of these will make classroom display

- Pairwork/dialogues

Resources
- Worksheets Set 2, 1–3
- Body flashcards
- *Aua!* flashcard
- Speech bubbles, template 7

- Pictures or photographs of people

Assignments
Classroom display (humorous?) of ailments, e.g. set out as a doctor's waiting room queue

Module 8: Enjoying life

8(i) Favourite pastimes

There is a lot of vocabulary here, although not all of it is new, and many words are cognates. Pupils should practise as many items as possible even if they will eventually choose only four or five for their own use. An attempt has been made to group the vocabulary into more manageable blocks and to keep the number of verbs needed as low as possible.

It may be best to introduce the phrases first without using *gern/nicht so gern* to help pupils understand the change in meaning and to avoid errors such as *Ich gern Tennis* (pupils often treat *gern* as a verb).

- Link phrases with pictures using cue cards and the worksheets Set 1.
- Play matching games such as dominoes to reinforce new vocabulary.
- When re-introducing likes and dislikes you may want to limit pairwork activities to *Spielst du gern. . . ?* and/or *Gehst du gern. . . ?* For the survey, allow pupils to choose the questions and hobbies they are most comfortable with.
- Pupils can also build up a personal profile of their likes and dislikes using their own design with the appropriate heart symbols.
- The suggested posters, suitably labelled, can serve as a classroom display, and so provide help with the vocabulary for the rest of the module.

Assignments

- Labelled picture profile illustrating personal interests.
- Class survey with findings presented in form of a bar chart; database; follow-up oral and written work. *Wieviele Personen spielen gern Tennis?* etc. The sample can be a small group rather than the whole class, to make it more manageable. Pupils will need to fill in the names of the people in the group and the sports/activities chosen for the survey. Some could survey sports, and some other activities to limit the size of the survey.
- The cassette could be either an interview (pairwork) or an individual oral profile of interests.

8(ii) Going out with friends

- Revise *Ich gehe. . .* from topic (i) using mime, flashcards, etc. Add the *Kommst du mit?* card to make up the whole invitation. Play 'Spot the rule' or similar to give pupils plenty of opportunity for practice and allowing them to hear the responses to the invitations before they use them themselves. Support your responses (*Oh ja, (gern)/Ach, nein danke*) by holding up an appropriate flashcard if necessary.

- If you want pupils to make dialogues where they decline an invitation and express a preference for a different activity, e.g. *Nein danke, ich gehe lieber. . .* use worksheet Set 3, Sheet 5a.
- Revise the time, full hours and maybe half hours but keep it simple.
- Use flashcards to practise *bei mir/bei dir*. It is possible to introduce a little more variety *Am Bus/Am Kino/Am Schwimmbad*, if pupils can manage it.
- When you have finally built up the whole conversation, sit pupils back to back and encourage them to use a prop to act out the telephone conversation, if necessary with the help of a prompt card.

Assignment

Pupils make up their own conversations with prompt cards. These conversations can be recorded on cassette or video.

Dialogue pattern (guidance only)

- *Tracy Smith, hallo?*
- *Hallo Tracy, hier ist die Vicky. Ich gehe ins Kino, kommst du mit?*
- *Ja, gern. Wann?*
- *Um 4 Uhr.*
- *Okay, gut. Und wo (treffen wir uns)?*
- *Bei mir?*
- *Ja, prima. Um 4 Uhr bei dir. Tschüß.*
- *Okay, tschüß.*

8(iii) Parts of the body

- Basic activities are as in the introduction for the presentation of new vocabulary.
- Playing *Walter sagt* is a fun, active way of involving the pupils in word recognition.

Assignment

- From *Walter sagt*, simple exercise routines can be built up. Pupils could work on individual routines, using keyboard rhythms or well-known tunes.
- Cut-outs from magazines – pupils can either be free to cut out the pictures they need to build up their collage person or directions can be given to guide them, e.g. *bitte einen Arm (ausschneiden)*, etc.
- When the collages are made they can be labelled and the display will reinforce vocabulary for the next topic.
- Both parts of the assignment have been gradually built up during the topic.

8(iv) Health

- Use mime and facial expression to present . . . *tut weh*.
- Pupils can come out to the front of the class in groups to mime the doctor's waiting-room queue with others in the class saying the words.
- Using a packet of cheap sticking plasters or Post-it stickers cut into strips, pupils put a plaster on a picture and give the appropriate utterance.
- This can become a written exercise if they then complete speech bubbles to go with each picture.
- Build up to simple conversations like this one:
  Tag, Tracy! Wie geht's?
  Ach, nicht so gut.
  (Nein?) Was ist los?
  Mein Hals tut weh!
  Oh je!/Ach du Arme! (Gute Besserung!). Tschüß.
  Danke, tschüß.
- Pupils can also make conversations linking topic (ii) with topic (iv) i.e.
  Ich gehe schwimmen, kommst du mit?
  Nein, ich kann nicht. Mein Bein tut weh.
- Use worksheet Set 2, Sheet 5a.

Assignment

From the above activities a queue of people (cut-outs or drawings) with their ailments can make a humorous classroom display.

MODULE 9 Being a teenager

Timescale
1 term

Areas of experience
A   D

Topics / Communicative objectives

Topics	Communicative objectives
(i) Pocket money	Exchanging information about how money is earned
(ii) Spending my money	Exchanging information about how money is spent
(iii) Clothes	Understanding and naming common items of clothing
	Exchanging information about what you like wearing

Assignments
Survey on spending habits

– Poster

– Scrapbook

– Tape

– Montage

– Magazine

this module allows the opportunity for an end of Key Stage creative product; ideally, individuals or groups work on their selected project connected with how they spend their money *Teenager heute*: sections could include '*Was sie tragen*'; '*Was sie essen*', '*Was sie hören*', '*Lieblingsspiele*', '*Lieblingstiere*', '*Lieblingsfarben*', etc. with titles, pictures and captions, survey results in tables/graphs/sentences, collages, poems, acrostics, wordsearches

Programme of study (part 1): Examples
1   Communicating in the target language
 (a) communicate with each other in pairs and groups and with the teacher
 (c) develop understanding and skills through a range of language activities
 (f) discuss own interests and compare them with those of others
2   Language skills
 (a) listen attentively for gist and detail
3   Language learning skills and knowledge of language
 (a) learn by heart phrases and short extracts
4   Cultural awareness
 (a) work with authentic materials

Cross-curricular opportunities

Money	Maths
Myself, my needs, how I spend my money	PSE

Opportunities for assessment: Examples

Respond to flashcards	AT1:1, AT2:1
Understand names of clothes	AT1:1
Understand how other people spend their money	AT1:2,3
Ask/answer questions on spending	AT1:1,2; AT2:1,2
Ask/answer survey questions	AT1:1,2; AT2:1,2,3
Say how you spend money	AT2:2,3
Matching words/pictures (clothes/leisure)	AT3:1,2
Match pictures to description	AT3:1,2,3
Label pictures	AT4:1,2
Write a few sentences about picture/own spending	AT4:2,3

Module 9 Being a teenager

Topic (i) Pocket money

Topic

(i) Pocket money

Communicative objective

Exchanging information about how money is earned

Linguistic objectives (examples)

Kriegst du Taschengeld?

Ja, . . . Pfund pro Woche.
            pro Monat.

Nein, (ich kriege kein Taschengeld).

Verdienst du Geld?

Ich habe einen Job.

Ich trage Zeitungen aus/Ich bin Zeitungsträger.

Ich helfe im Haus.
          im Garten.

Ich mache Babysitting/Ich bin Babysitter.

Wieviel Geld hast du pro Monat?

Ich habe. . . Pfund.

(Was,) so viel?

(Was,) so wenig?

Numbers (as appropriate)

Activities

- Presentation with coins, numbers and flashcards
- Worksheets Set 1, 1–4
- OHP games/noughts and crosses
- Miming
- Matching words and pictures
- Counting money
- Questions and answers
- Pairwork – worksheet Set 2, 5a; groupwork

Resources

- Worksheets Set 1, 1–4
- Household task flashcards
- Number sheets
- Various flashcards linked with this topic
- Noughts and crosses, templates 3a and 3b, e.g. with jobs for pocket money
- German name cards, template 15
- Cue cards

- Number cards
- Imitation money
- Pictures of people
- Song cassette

Assignments

The topic works towards the final assignment – see page 155

It could begin as a survey on how money is earned

Module: 9 Being a teenager

Topic (ii) Spending my money

Topic
(ii) Spending my money

Communicative objective
Exchanging information about how money
is spent

Linguistic objectives (examples)
Was machst du mit dem Geld?

Ich kaufe   Bonbons (und Schokolade).

Kassetten.

CDs.

Zeitschriften.

Kleider.

Kosmetika.

Geschenke.

Ich gehe   aus.

in die Disko.

ins Kino.

ins Schwimmbad.

zum Fußball.

zu Popkonzerten.

Das ist teuer!
Das ist billig!/Das ist nicht teuer!

Activities
- Flashcard presentation/games
- Matching cue cards
- Recognizing and saying prices
- Listening and matching prices to items, Worksheet Set 3, 3
- Choosing realistic prices for items, worksheet Set 1, 4
- Discussing dear/cheap
- Class survey
- Song

Resources
- Worksheets Set 1, 4, Set 2, 1–3, Set 3, 3
- Various flashcards
- Made-up wordsearch, template 4b
- Noughts and crosses, templates 3a and 3b
- Pelmanism/snap, template 1
- Survey sheet, template 10
- Cue cards

- Price cards
- Song cassette

Assignments
Survey on spending habits (made into illustrated pie chart)

Module 9 Being a teenager

Topic (iii) Clothes

Topic
(iii) Clothes

Communicative objective
Understanding and naming common items of clothing

Linguistic objectives (examples)

Ich trage. . .

Er/Sie trägt. . .

die Jeans (-)

das T-shirt (-s)

das Sweatshirt (-s)

die Shorts (-)

das Kleid (-er)

der Rock (¨e)

die Jacke (-n)

der Schlips (-e)

das Hemd (-en)

der Pullover (der Pulli) (-), (-s)

die Bluse (-n)

die Mütze (-n)

die Schuhe (pl)

die Socken (pl)

die Stiefel (pl)

die Sportschuhe (pl)

Numbers 1–100

Activities

• Flashcard presentation

• Building up outfits on OHT

• Worksheets Set 1, 1–4

• Wordsearch

• Matching games – matching prices to clothes, discussing if they are cheap or expensive

• Pupils say what a person in a magazine picture is wearing

• Matching pictures with descriptions

• Bingo – clothes in suitcase

• Song

• Pupils list/draw and label their own or their ideal wardrobe.

Resources

• Worksheets Set 1, 1–4

• Clothes flashcards

• Pelmanism/snap, template 1

• Dominoes, template 2

• Bingo, template B11

• Made-up wordsearch, template 4b

• OHT clothes, cut out from picture sheets

• Cue cards

• Number sheets, templates 15a and 15b

• Prices

• Clothes

• Magazine pictures of clothes

• Song cassette

Assignments

Poster

Scrapbook

Tape

Montage

Magazine

this module allows the opportunity for an end of Key Stage creative product; ideally, individuals or groups work on their selected project connected with how they spend their money

Fashion show – pupils can introduce their own or each other's actual or ideal outfits

Ideal outfit and costing (not related to actual spending power). Ideal outfit could be drawn or made up from collage of magazine pictures

Module 9: Being a teenager

9(i) Pocket money

How much? (money and numbers)
- Revise 1–20 in a variety of ways.
- Use plastic pound coins or tokens to give out; pupils say how much money they have: *Wieviel Geld hast du?* Encourage class to respond to the sums of money they have heard: *Was, so viel?/Was, so wenig?* This could also be a small group activity where each pupil says how much money she/he has and with other group members responding.
- Move on to how much pocket money they receive.
- German name cards or pictures from magazines could be linked with amounts of money: *Er/sie* (or name) *hat (kriegt). . . Mark.*

How much money is earned – vocabulary
- Present flashcards for how money is earned.
- Mimes can reinforce this vocabulary.
- Then Worksheets Set 1 and OHT noughts and crosses will give more practice.
- Sentence-building can be done on the board or OHP with pictures of people or their names, and amounts of money and speech bubbles for pupils to say how it is earned.

How money is earned – exchange of information
- Initially teacher can ask question: *Bist du Zeitungsträger?* with single *ja/nein* response.
- Then go on to *Was machst du. . . ?* question encouraging a full answer.
- Then pairwork can be used to exchange information.

9(ii) Spending my money
- Revise the vocabulary for going to places.
- Introduce vocabulary for items purchased using flashcards/OHT, etc.
- Have price cards for pupils to say prices they see. Careful – you are here using **English** prices since pupils are shopping in England.
- A wordsearch will reinforce words.
- Noughts and crosses can be used to get pupils to put correct verbs, i.e. *Ich gehe/Ich kaufe* with images given.

Discussing prices
- Price activity as above.

- Price cards can be put with flashcards for pupils to learn *Das ist (nicht) teuer/Das ist billig.*
- Worksheet Set 3, 3 can be made for pupils to listen for prices of items.
- Worksheets Set 2 will help pupils to write down information from hearing items and prices and could also be given with items and prices for pupils to comment in writing *Das ist teuer/Das ist billig.*
- Snap card sized pictures can be given out to pupils (four or five each) with an equal number of relevant prices to help them learn to put realistic prices on items.

Assignment
- The survey will give ample speaking/listening/recording practice in a realistic activity.

9(iii) Clothes
- Flashcard/cue card presentation of new vocabulary.
- OHT cut-outs can build up outfits.
- Worksheets Set 1 and wordsearch will reinforce vocabulary.
- Any of the matching games can be used here.
- Beetle will build up outfits; Kim's game will help memorize vocabulary.
- Magazine cut-outs can be used for pupils to list the clothes worn.
- Pupils can be given actual clothes to dress up in or simply to name. This could be followed by a 'silly fashion show' (or a serious one) with a commentary on what people are wearing.

Price of clothes
- Higher numbers can be taught (60–100 included if pupils can cope with these).
- The same levels of activity as in 9(ii) can be done matching prices and clothes, discussing relative value for money, etc.

Assignment
- The final assignment suggestion on clothes, with either cut-outs or pupils' own illustrations, is a necessary alternative to discussions of money for those who receive little or none. The outfit can be costed so that the element of money is still included.

157

Module 1: Vocabulary

das Lineal	das Papier	das Buch	das Heft
die Tafel	das Fenster	das Bild	der Spitzer
der Stuhl	der Tisch	die Tür	die Schultasche
der Filzstift	der Radiergummi	der Kuli	der Bleistift
schreiben	setzen	aufstehen	Ruhe bitte!
nachsprechen	hören	lesen	abschreiben kopieren
fragen	malen	raten	spielen
nehmen	zeigen	gucken	antworten

    DEUTSCH? KEIN PROBLEM!

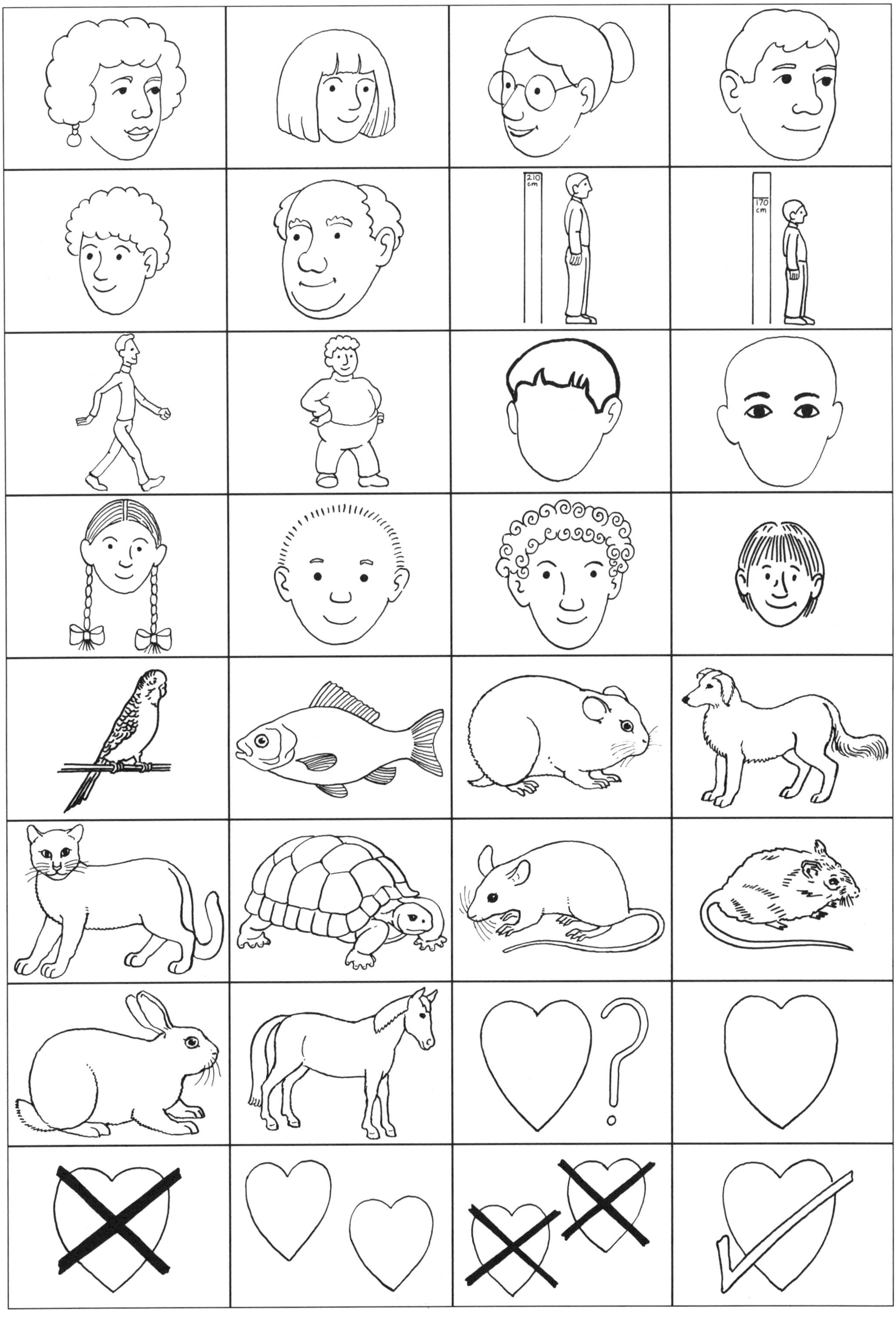
210 cm
170 cm

mein Vater	meine Großmutter/Oma	meine Schwester	meine Mutter
klein	groß	mein Großvater/Opa	mein Bruder
die Augen	die Haare	vollschlank	schlank
glatte Haare	lockige Haare	kurze Haare	lange Haare
der Hund	der Hamster	der Goldfisch	der Vogel
die Springmaus	die Maus	die Schildkröte	die Katze
Ich mag	Magst du?	das Pferd	das Kaninchen
Ich mag lieber	Ich hasse	Ich liebe	Ich mag keine

161

Naturwissenschaft Biologie Physik Chemie	Deutsch	Mathe(matik)	Englisch
Musik	Religion	Erdkunde	Geschichte
Theater	Kunst	Technik Werken	Sport
			Informatik
doof	leicht einfach	interessant	toll
	schwierig	langweilig	schrecklich
die Pause	nach	vor	der Stundenplan
	nachmittags	vormittags	die Mittagspause

die Schule	die Kantine	das Schulbüro	die Bücherei
der Chemiesaal	die Turnhalle die Sporthalle	der Schulhof	der Gang der Korridor
	der Sportplatz	das Klassenzimmer	die Anmeldung
Gehen Sie hier links	Gehen Sie hier rechts	links	rechts
			Gehen Sie hier geradeaus

das Haus	der Garten	die Garage	die Wohnung
an der Küste	auf dem Land	in einem Dorf	in der Stadt
in Frankfurt	in Plymouth	in Deutschland	in Großbritannien in England in Schottland
	der Balkon	in der Nähe von. . .	in. . .
das Zimmer	die Treppe	die Küche	das Schlafzimmer
die Toilette	das Wohnzimmer	das Badezimmer	das Eßzimmer
links von	rechts von		die Terrasse
gegenüber	neben	oben im ersten Stock	unten im Erdgeschoß

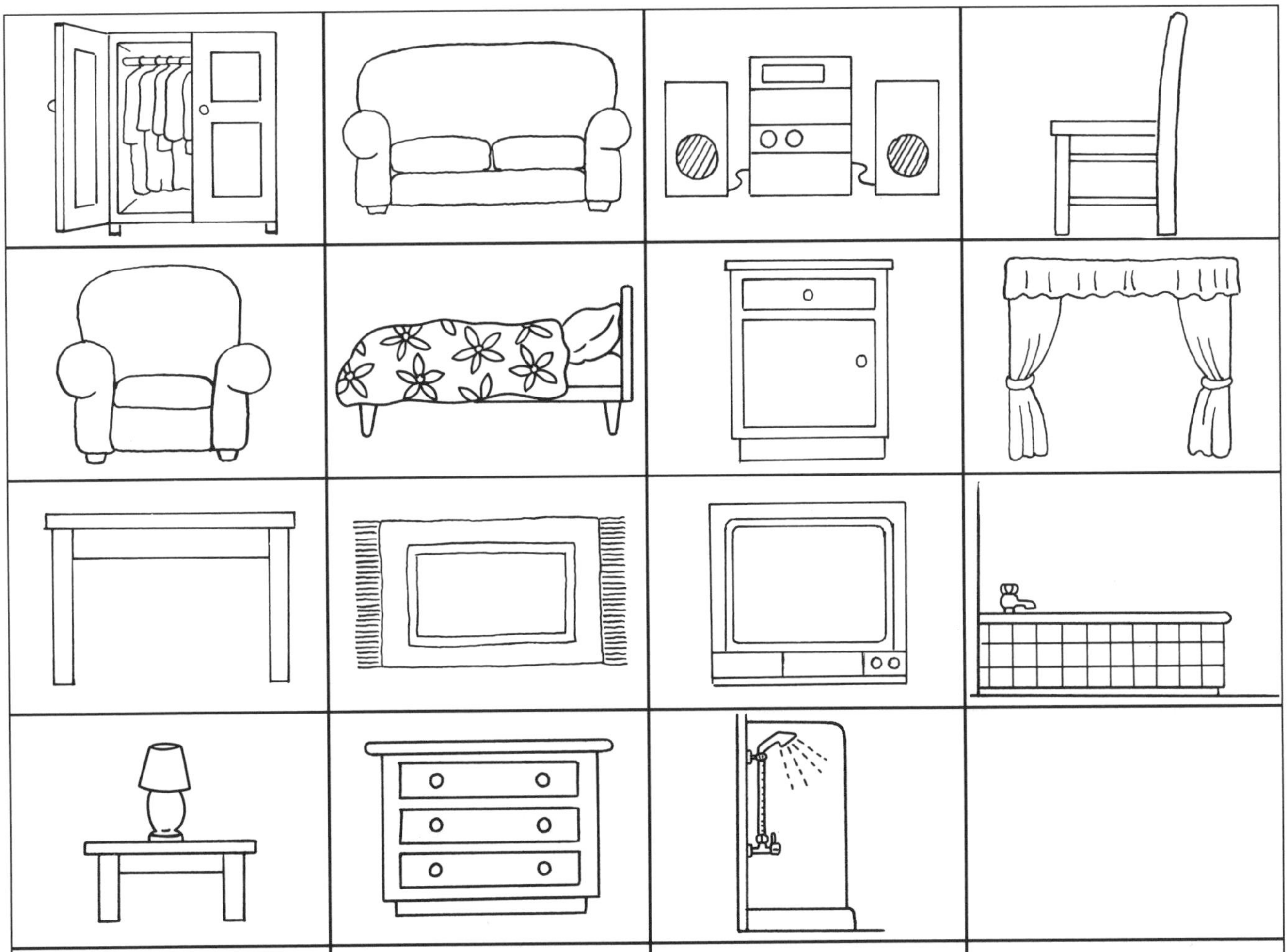

der Stuhl	die HIFI-Anlage	das Sofa	der Kleiderschrank
die Gardinen die Vorhänge	der Schrank	das Bett	der Sessel
die Badewanne	der Fernseher	der Teppich	der Tisch
	die Dusche	die Kommode	die Lampe

DEUTSCH? KEIN PROBLEM!

mit dem Bus	ich fliege	mit der Fähre	mit dem Zug
Schweiz	Österreich	Deutschland	mit dem Auto
das Geschäft der Laden	das Einkaufszentrum		England
die Apotheke	die Konditorei	der Zeitungsladen	der Schnellimbiß die Imbißstube
der Supermarkt	der Markt	die Metzgerei	die Bäckerei
der Käse	der Schinken	das Brot	das Brötchen
eine Mark	ein Pfennig	deutsches Geld	
	ein Zwanzigmarkschein	ein Zehnmarkschein	ein Fünfmarkstück

DEUTSCH? KEIN PROBLEM!

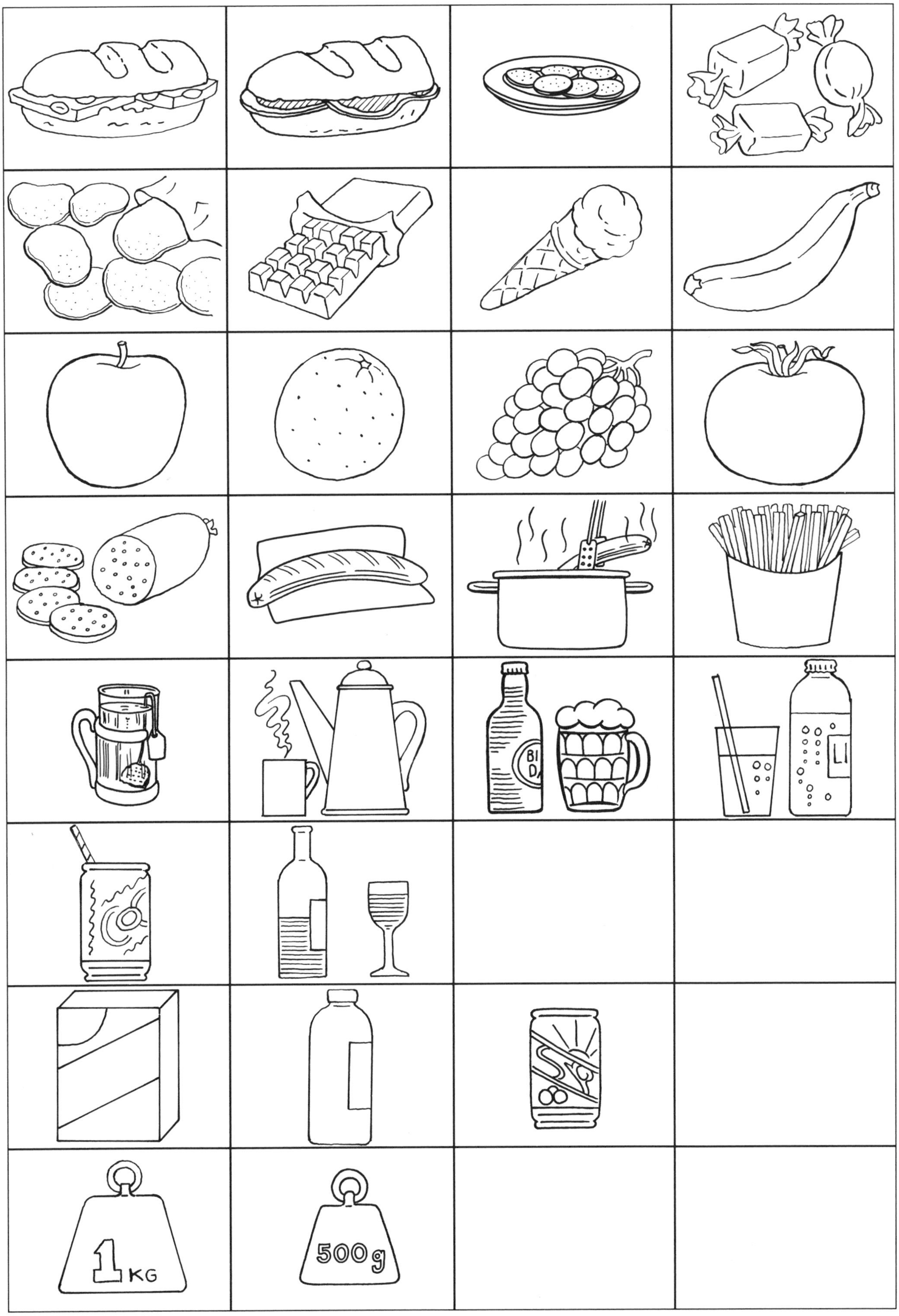
1 KG
500g

die Bonbons	die Kekse	das Schinkenbrötchen	das Käsebrot
die Banane	das Eis	die Schokolade	die Kartoffelchips
die Tomate	die Trauben	die Apfelsine die Orange	der Apfel
die Pommes frites	die Bockwurst	die Bratwurst	die Wurst
die Limonade	das Bier	der Kaffee	der Tee
		der Wein	das Cola
	eine Dose	eine Flasche	eine Packung
		ein Pfund	ein Kilo zwei Pfund

    DEUTSCH? KEIN PROBLEM!

173

arbeitet im Garten	hört Musik	sieht fern	macht Sport
liest	geht tanzen	bastelt am Auto	spielt mit dem Computer
macht das Geschirr	macht die Wäsche	macht die Betten	macht sauber
		macht die Einkäufe	macht das Essen

     DEUTSCH? KEIN PROBLEM!

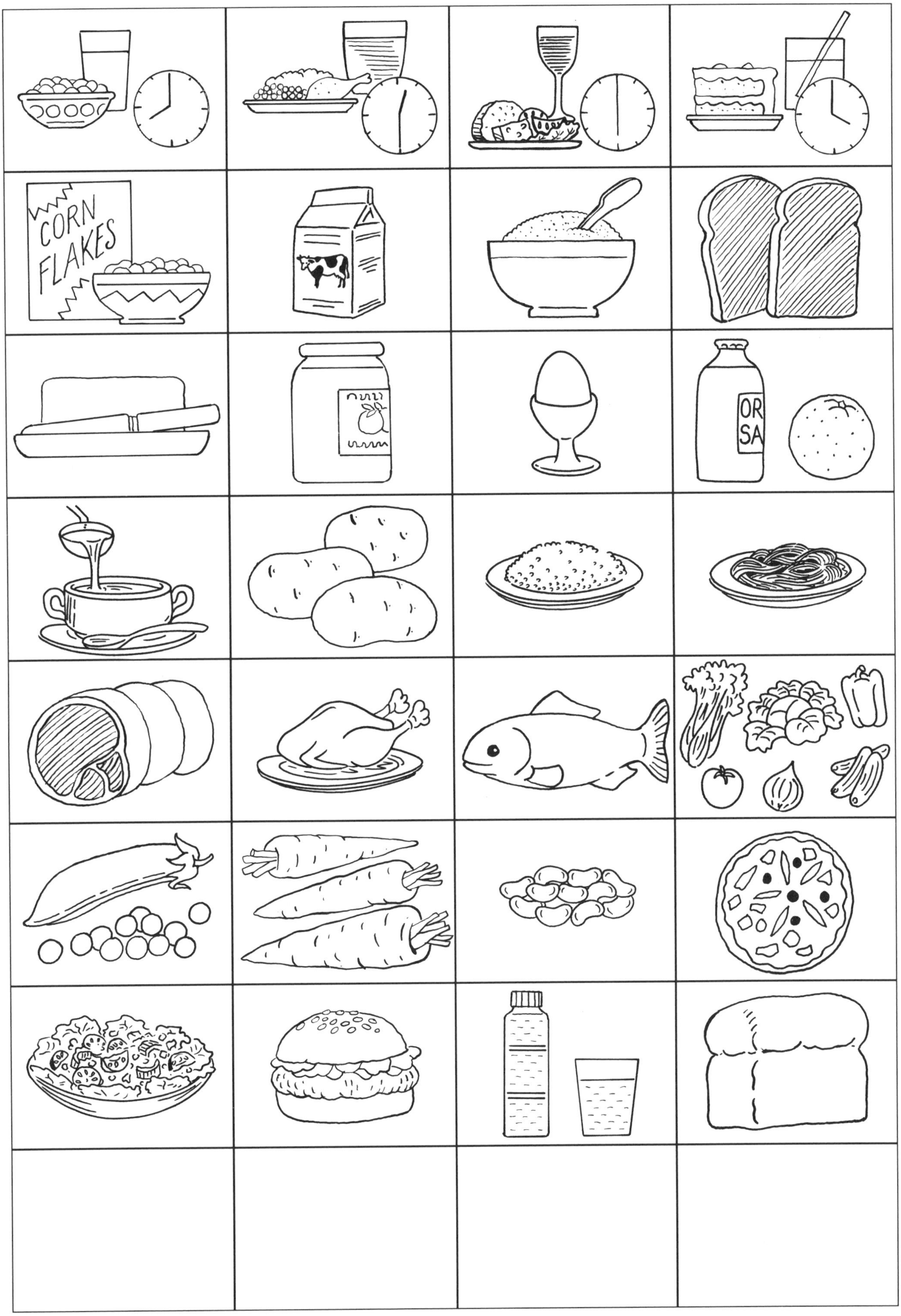
CORN FLAKES
OR SA

Module 6: Vocabulary

zwischendurch	das Abendessen das Abendbrot	das Mittagessen	das Frühstück
der Toast	der Zucker	die Milch	die Cornflakes
der Orangensaft	ein Ei	die Marmelade	die Butter
die Nudeln	der Reis	die Kartoffeln	die Suppe
das Gemüse	der Fisch	das Hähnchen	das Fleisch
die Pizza	die Bohnen	die Karotten	die Erbsen
das Brot	das Wasser	der Hamburger	der Salat

 　　　　　　　　　　　　　　　DEUTSCH? KEIN PROBLEM!

© *John Murray (Publishers) Ltd* **177**

die Disko(thek)	das Kino	das Sportzentrum	das Café
das Eisstadion	der Park	das Museum	die Geschäfte
die Altstadt	der Hafen	der Strand	das Schwimmbad
das Stadion	mit dem Fahrrad	zu Fuß	
			das Restaurant

Badminton	Snooker	am Wochenende	abends
Tennis	Rugby	Fußball	Basketball
reiten	malen	radfahren	einkaufen
tanzen	mit dem Computer spielen	angeln	der Kopf
der Mund	die Nase	das Auge	das Ohr
der Rücken	der Finger	der Körper	der Arm
die Hand	das Bein	der Hals	das Knie
der Zahn (die Zähne)	mein(e). . . tut weh Aua!	der Bauch	der Fuß

	Ich bin Babysitter. Ich mache Babysitting.	Ich habe einen Job.	Ich bin Zeitungsträger. Ich trage Zeitungen aus.
die CDs	die Kassetten	die Geschenke	die Kosmetika
Ich gehe zu Popkonzerten.	die Schokolade	Ich gehe zum Fußball.	die Zeitschriften
die Schuhe	die Socken		die Kleider
der Rock	die Jeans	der Schlips	das Hemd
das T-shirt	die Shorts	das Kleid	der Pullover der Pulli
die Mütze	die Bluse	die Sportschuhe	die Jacke
		die Stiefel	das Sweatshirt

 DEUTSCH? KEIN PROBLEM!